AN UNCONVENTIONAL BRIDE

FENELLA J. MILLER

Boldwood

First published in 2017. This edition published in Great Britain in 2025 by Boldwood Books Ltd.

Copyright © Fenella J. Miller, 2017

Cover Design by Colin Thomas

Cover Images: Colin Thomas and iStock

The moral right of Fenella J. Miller to be identified as the author of this work has been asserted in accordance with the Copyright, Designs and Patents Act 1988.

All rights reserved. No part of this book may be reproduced in any form or by any electronic or mechanical means, including information storage and retrieval systems, without written permission from the author, except for the use of brief quotations in a book review. This book is a work of fiction and, except in the case of historical fact, any resemblance to actual persons, living or dead, is purely coincidental.

Every effort has been made to obtain the necessary permissions with reference to copyright material, both illustrative and quoted. We apologise for any omissions in this respect and will be pleased to make the appropriate acknowledgements in any future edition.

A CIP catalogue record for this book is available from the British Library.

Paperback ISBN 978-1-83678-314-5

Large Print ISBN 978-1-83678-315-2

Hardback ISBN 978-1-83678-313-8

Ebook ISBN 978-1-83678-316-9

Kindle ISBN 978-1-83678-317-6

Audio CD ISBN 978-1-83678-308-4

MP3 CD ISBN 978-1-83678-309-1

Digital audio download ISBN 978-1-83678-312-1

This book is printed on certified sustainable paper. Boldwood Books is dedicated to putting sustainability at the heart of our business. For more information please visit https://www.boldwoodbooks.com/about-us/sustainability/

Boldwood Books Ltd, 23 Bowerdean Street, London, SW6 3TN

www.boldwoodbooks.com

1

FEBRUARY 1813, SILCHESTER COURT

'Forgive me, your grace, this letter has arrived by express.' The butler bowed deeply and held out the silver salver.

'Thank you, Peebles.' Beau scanned the letter and was so startled by the contents he sent his coffee cup flying from the table.

Already this year was turning out to be an unmitigated disaster. First Peregrine, the oldest by five minutes of the twins, had bought himself a set of colours and was at this very moment undergoing some rudimentary training before being shipped out to the Peninsula to fight for King and Country. Why in God's name Perry had felt the need to become a soldier he'd no idea. Perhaps it was because Bennett had had a successful career in the military until he resigned his commission when their father had died.

Aubrey had taken his brother's departure badly and was mooching around the house, unable to settle on anything. The twins had done everything together and Beau supposed he must be grateful that both hadn't taken the king's shilling.

Giselle had slipped on the ice and broken her leg two months ago. She still insisted she was unable to walk and was therefore marooned upstairs in her rooms. Perhaps this letter was not such bad news after all.

He looked at the letter again and smiled. He tucked it into his waistcoat pocket and went in search of his brother. Aubrey spent a lot of the day with Giselle in her apartment. She was missing Madeline, indeed they all were, since her older sister had married Lord Carshalton last year. The fact that Giselle also had to postpone her Season until next year had added to her low spirits.

Beau took the stairs two at a time and walked straight into his sister's sitting room. His siblings were staring morosely into the fire, not even engaged in desultory conversation.

'I have just received a letter from a relative of our mother's.' This announcement caught their attention as no one in the family had known they had any other relatives.

'Who is it? Are they coming to visit?' Giselle said, a welcome spark of interest in her eyes.

He flicked back his coat-tails and settled beside her on the *chaise longue*. 'Do you remember Mama telling us that her sister married a younger son of the Earl of Guildford?'

She shook her head but Aubrey nodded. 'I think you must have been too young, Giselle, but I do recall hearing that story. Didn't they go to India and perish in some uprising or other?'

'That's what Mama was led to believe. However, it seems there was a child, a girl, who eventually found her way to these shores and has been living quietly somewhere in Somerset. Elizabeth Freemantle is our cousin's name, and she is now seventeen years of age and it seems that I am responsible for her. She wishes to be presented.'

'Beau, please don't leave me here alone. I couldn't bear it. It's bad enough not being able to go to London myself...'

An Unconventional Bride

He reached across and patted her sound knee. 'Don't fret, little one, I've no intention of going myself. I rather thought that Aubrey could do it in my stead. The house in Grosvenor Square is already prepared and fully staffed as we expected to be up there for your come-out.'

His brother looked dubious. 'Let me get this straight, brother – you want me to do the pretty with my cousin? Escort her to dozens of routs, soirées and balls? That doesn't sound too shabby.'

'You can't possibly do it, Aubrey – at three and twenty, you're far too young. The poor girl would be better off waiting until next year when Beau can take charge and escort us both,' Giselle argued.

This was exactly the response he'd been hoping for from his sister. Like all the males in this family his brother couldn't resist a challenge.

'If Perry is old enough to fight then I am certainly old enough to act as sponsor to our unknown cousin. Can I see the letter for myself, Beau? I think you are keeping something back from us.'

Beau handed it to him. His brother read the missive out loud:

Dear Duke of Silchester,

You do not know me and no doubt will be wondering why a stranger has the effrontery to send a letter by express. I am writing on behalf of your cousin, Miss Elizabeth Freemantle, the orphaned child of your aunt, Lady Elizabeth Freemantle. I only recently discovered that she is your cousin and that you are her legal guardian. If I had realised this earlier I would have sent her to you immediately.

It is possible, of course, that you were unaware of the existence of your cousin. When her parents died in India you might

> *well have assumed that their baby, Elizabeth, perished also. I was able to save the child and have been taking care of her since then. I was entrusted with not only the baby but also her fortune.*
>
> *My husband, Captain Cassidy, was an officer in the East India Company and we were also stationed in India. He too was killed by the insurgents. I fled with Elizabeth, and my own daughter Mary, and made my way to Somerset, where we have resided ever since.*
>
> *Miss Freemantle is a considerable heiress and will be in much demand on the marriage mart. I heard on good authority that her youngest cousin, Lady Giselle, is to make her come-out this Season and, obviously, Miss Freemantle will be presented with her.*
>
> *My own daughter, Mrs Mary Williams, will accompany Miss Freemantle as her companion. She was widowed three years ago when her husband was killed.*
>
> *Miss Freemantle is now seventeen years of age, well-educated and spirited. She will do better in the charge of a gentleman like yourself. She is travelling with my daughter and man of business, and will be at Silchester Court by the end of the week. Mr Gregson will hand to you the necessary papers and legal documents.*
>
> *I am in uncertain health and being responsible for Miss Freemantle is something I can no longer do.*

His brother shook his head. 'This girl is going to be foisted off on us without a by-your-leave? Reading between the lines, Beau, I think Mrs Cassidy is glad to get shot of her. For the word "spirited" I think we could substitute "wild".'

Giselle was having none of this. 'How can you say that about our cousin? I'm absolutely thrilled she's joining the family. Does that mean you will send Aubrey and Cousin Elizabeth away in April?'

'If you would make more of an effort to get about, sweetheart, then maybe we could all go as originally planned? However, if you don't get on your feet by the end of March, Aubrey shall go with Elizabeth and her companion, and you must remain on your own with me.'

For a moment he thought he'd gone too far, that she would dissolve into tears at his harsh words. Instead she pursed her lips and nodded. 'I have allowed my sadness at losing my sister and two brothers to keep me languishing up here. From now on I shall come down to dinner and begin to exercise my leg as the doctor told me to.'

Mission accomplished Beau left them in animated discussion about the possible character and appearance of this new member of the family. He had a nasty suspicion Aubrey was correct – the young lady in question was going to be a handful. His lips curved. He was thirteen years her senior and had no doubt whatsoever he would curb whatever tendencies she might have to misbehave.

* * *

'Help me get up, Aubrey. I'm going to begin practising walking immediately. It's quite possible I've lost the use of my legs having malingered here for so long.'

'Up you come, sister, but you mustn't overdo it.' He kept his arm around her waist and gently assisted her to her feet. She only managed half a dozen steps before complaining that her leg hurt too much to continue.

'Of course it does, you goose, but I insist that you walk the length of this room and back before you give up. Beau means it –

he will send us without you. Surely you cannot wish to miss the excitement of your first Season?'

She pulled a face but did as he asked. By the time they reached the windows she was walking more freely. 'It is painful, but I feel so much better being upright and not being carried around like an unwanted parcel.'

He returned her to her position on the daybed and stepped back. For the first time since Perry had left he began to feel more cheerful. 'I'm going down to talk to Beau. I'll be back to escort you to dinner this afternoon.' He reached the door and then turned back. 'No doubt Elizabeth will require a new wardrobe – why don't you send a letter to your modiste? I'm sure you won't want to be eclipsed by a girl two years younger than you.'

This was exactly the motivation his sister needed. 'Thank you for reminding me. I shall write immediately. She must send me the latest fashion plates and samples of material so we have something to choose from.'

He raised a hand in casual salute and headed downstairs. As he arrived in the vast entrance hall the door opened and Bennett stepped in, looking remarkably pleased with himself.

Aubrey jumped the remaining stairs in one go and ran across to embrace his brother. 'Is Grace not with you? We have such exciting news to impart. Both she and Madeline will be quite astounded.'

'I don't believe anything you can tell me will eclipse the news I have to give you. Grace is with child and in September you will become an uncle for the first time.'

'You must come with me and tell Beau. He will be as delighted as I am.'

Bennett and Beau could be twins, like he and Perry, so similar in appearance were they. The news that they had a cousin called Elizabeth was discussed at length.

'I'm going up to tell Giselle my good news. Grace is with Madeline – I shouldn't be surprised if there will be not one, but two new arrivals this year.'

'Make that three, Bennett. Elizabeth is also a new member of the family – albeit a fully grown one.'

Aubrey remained with his older brother. 'I know none of us are sticklers for protocol, but will this companion, Mrs Williams, be sufficient to silence the tabbies? Should we not find an older woman to act as chaperone to the girls?'

His brother looked at him as if he was speaking in tongues. 'One middle-aged woman in the household is more than sufficient without fetching in another. God's teeth! It is perfectly proper for us to reside under the same roof as our cousin.'

'I suppose so. She's also your ward, which would give her double protection. I've probably spent more time in Town during the Season than anyone else. Don't forget that Perry and I have experienced two Seasons already.'

'Quite true – I tend to avoid London during the months of April to June for that very reason. The more I think about it, little brother, the more convinced I am that you should oversee this project. I will, of course, be there for Giselle and Elizabeth's come-out ball – but will remain here as much as possible.'

'Let's hope our cousin will not prove to be a confirmed flirt. I'm going to have my work cut out keeping the rakehells and fortune hunters away if she is as pretty as either of our sisters, especially as she has a massive fortune.'

'I have every faith in you, Aubrey. Don't forget you will have the assistance of this Mrs Williams. The fact that she is prepared to remain at the side of her adopted sister must mean the girl cannot be that bad.'

* * *

'Elizabeth Freemantle, if you continue to behave like a spoilt brat I shall cancel our journey to Hertfordshire and you will remain cloistered with me and Mama for another year.' Mary's patience was running out. 'I can assure you that his grace is not eager to assume responsibility for you and will be only too happy to postpone your arrival indefinitely.'

This was a fabrication, but if he did know exactly what he was letting himself in for she was certain he would echo her words.

'Oh do not say so, dearest Mary, I promise I shall be good.' The girl – for in all honesty Mary couldn't think of her as a woman grown, even though she was seventeen years of age – smiled and if she didn't know any better she would have been deceived by the angelic expression.

Elizabeth was just above average height, had a delightful figure, golden curls and periwinkle blue eyes. In fact, she was as beautiful as she was rich – a lethal combination for any gentleman.

'You must give me your word, Beth, that there will be no more tantrums. Not only is it unbecoming in a young lady to stamp and scream as you just did, but it is also behaviour that will not endear you to your new family.' She had the full attention of her charge now. 'His grace, from what I have gleaned, is a formidable gentleman and expects those around him to match his impeccable manners. I'm certain that at the slightest sign of misbehaviour from you he will refuse to take you to London.'

'But he would not send me back here? Even if I angered him he would keep me at Silchester Court?'

This was the first sign of genuine remorse and Mary took pity on the girl. 'He has accepted that he is now your legal guardian and I'm sure will take his responsibilities seriously. However, my dear, I suggest that you keep your temper in check as you might find yourself soundly beaten.'

This last threat reduced Beth to tears. The girl had never had a cross word directed at her and certainly no hand had been raised to check her wild behaviour. 'I will be very good; I give you my solemn promise. You will not leave me there alone, will you, Mary?'

'I shall stay as long as you need me, but remember the duke can send me away at any time. Now, sweetheart, dry your eyes and continue with your packing.'

The tantrum had been caused when Mary had suggested the porcelain dolls should remain behind as they were the playthings of a child.

Beth removed the offending objects from the trunk and left her maid to complete the task uninterrupted.

* * *

Two days later they were on their way in a luxurious carriage. The luggage was in a separate vehicle a few hours ahead of them and Mr Gregson rode alongside. Mary's dresser, Jessie, and Beth's maid, Anna, were travelling with them.

Mary was still dubious about arriving uninvited at the home of one of the most prestigious gentlemen in the country. Mama had insisted this was the only way to be certain the duke would take over the responsibility for his cousin.

Beth was curled up in the corner, rugs across her sleeping form, without a care in the world. She left the worrying to those who took care of her. Her winning ways and stunning looks always got her what she wanted. Since she was fifteen there had been a constant stream of would-be suitors and it was only a matter of time before Beth threw her cap over the windmill and ran off with someone totally unsuitable.

It was because of this that Mary had taken charge and delved through the boxes of papers that pertained to the girl – something her mother should have done years ago. When she saw the marriage certificate of Beth's parents she realised the girl did not belong with them at all. There was someone who could protect the one the one she loved like a sister.

Once this information had been shared, her mother was adamant that Beth should leave at once and take her proper place in society. She had loved and spoiled her adopted daughter but now felt guilty she had denied Beth the things she was entitled to.

The journey from Somerset was tedious in the extreme and even Beth's enthusiasm was waning when they finally turned into the long drive that led to Silchester Court.

'Remember to curtsy, Beth, and only speak when you're spoken to. I think it would be wise to let your new family believe you are a docile and biddable young lady.'

Beth giggled. 'My behaviour will be impeccable, dearest Mary. They will think me not only pretty but also quiet and well behaved.' She reached up her gloved hand and touched the deep brim of her silk-lined bonnet. 'How long must I keep up this pretence before I reveal my true character?'

Mary laughed and the two maids hid their smiles behind their hands. 'You are incorrigible, my love, and I'm certain you will run rings around your cousins. You have six of them – do you recall their names or shall we go through them again?'

'The oldest of the six is the duke himself – he is unmarried. Next is Lord Sheldon – he is married. Then there are the twins, Lord Peregrine and Lord Aubrey – they too are unmarried. Lady Madeline is married and Lady Giselle is not.'

'You are a baggage, my dear, as I've often told you before. If you attempt to flirt with any of them…'

Beth rounded her eyes as if horrified by the suggestion. 'I'm not a widgeon; much as I would like to be married to a duke, he is far too old for me. And anyway, I believe that marriage between first cousins is not considered a good thing. They will be like brothers and sisters to me, nothing more.'

Mary wasn't fooled for an instant. Her volatile charge had already decided she was going to marry one of these gentlemen, whatever anybody said to the contrary.

2

The carriage rocked to a standstill in front of an impressive set of marble steps. Half a dozen liveried footmen were waiting in the turning circle to receive them, and a gentleman in black and a lady in navy waited at the top. Why the butler thought it necessary to send so many servants Mary had no idea.

'Are you ready, Beth?'

The girl frowned. 'Why is the duke not there to greet me?'

'I expect he has more important things to do, my dear. Until a few days ago he did not know of your existence and wasn't given any option about your arrival. I think that the welcome we *are* receiving is better than I expected.'

The carriage door was opened and the steps let down. As the junior member of the party Beth should have waited, but she stepped out first, leaving Mary to follow. The girl stalked, nose in the air, to the head of the steps and sailed past the two people waiting to introduce themselves.

There was nothing she could do but hurry on behind and hope her charge didn't offend anyone else before she was there to curb her. She paused and nodded at the butler and housekeeper.

'Good afternoon, madam, welcome to Silchester Court. I am Peebles, butler here, and this is Mrs Anderson, the housekeeper.'

Mary smiled but didn't speak. She knew better than to engage in idle conversation with servants. She stepped into a vast entrance hall and was horrified to see Beth had vanished. Where could the girl have gone in so short a space of time?

A tall, dark young man strode into view. 'I do beg your pardon, Mrs Williams, for not being here to greet you. I am Lord Aubrey Sheldon. My brother, the duke, has been unavoidably detained but hopefully will return tomorrow.' His smile was warm and his words genuine.

She didn't curtsy – she might not be an aristocrat but she was wealthy and impeccably bred and had no intention of being treated like an inferior being.

'I'm delighted to meet you, my lord. This might seem an odd question, but have you any notion where Miss Freemantle might be?'

Before he could answer the girl appeared in the gallery that overlooked the hall. 'I'm up here, Mary. I just couldn't resist having a look around.'

This was hardly an auspicious start. His lordship raised an eyebrow and looked distinctly unimpressed at this breach of etiquette.

'Come down immediately, Elizabeth, and make your curtsy to Lord Aubrey.'

Instead of doing as she was bid the girl waved and gave him her most winning smile. 'I might as well stay where I am. Is someone going to show me to my accommodation?'

Mary turned to Lord Aubrey. 'I apologise for Miss Freemantle's appalling lack of manners, my lord. I can assure you I shall have words with her. She knows better than this.'

'You are her companion, Mrs Williams, not her guardian. My

brother will soon put her straight.' He nodded politely and gestured to the housekeeper who was hovering anxiously nearby. 'Anderson, show Mrs Williams and Miss Freemantle to their chambers.' Then he strolled away without bidding her farewell.

If a younger member of the family was so toplofty then she dreaded to think what the duke would be like. She stared after him, tempted to call him back and put him straight on a few things. He obviously considered her a paid employee, which was not the case. Although her fortune was not equal to Beth's, she was sufficiently wealthy to pay her own way in the world and had inherited a substantial estate in Suffolk from her husband.

The only reason she had returned home after she had been widowed was to assist her mother. Even straight out of the schoolroom Beth was proving to be a handful. No expense had been spared in her upbringing and her every whim had been indulged. The magnificent estate where they had lived had been purchased from the money her father had left her.

Mary followed the housekeeper and was unsurprised, but decidedly put out, to discover that Beth's apartment was luxurious and in the family wing of this huge house, whereas her room was on the next floor and more suitable for a governess than someone of her standing.

She paused at the door but didn't go in. 'I do not intend to sleep here, Anderson. I believe you must be under a misapprehension. I am not a servant or employee – I am a guest. I shall return downstairs whilst you find me somewhere more suitable.'

The housekeeper looked horrified, as well she might. She curtsied. 'I do beg your pardon, Mrs Williams. I have indeed been misinformed. If you will follow me I shall take you to one of the guest suites. Your luggage will be transferred immediately.'

Mary nodded and stepped aside so the agitated woman could take her somewhere more appropriate to her station. The apartment she was ushered into was well appointed and comfortable. Unfortunately, the fires were not lit and the rooms were unpleasantly cold.

'I have no intention of remaining here until these rooms are habitable. Kindly direct me to a withdrawing room and have coffee and refreshments sent immediately.'

A lurking footman jumped to attention and at a nod from the housekeeper bowed to Mary. 'Would you care to follow me, ma'am?'

The chamber she was taken to was delightfully warm and exactly right for the purpose. She took a moment to admire the strutting peacocks that adorned two of the walls. She had yet to remove her outer garments. It wasn't done to take one's bonnet off oneself, but needs must. Whilst following the drum on the Peninsula she had learned to adapt to her circumstances and no longer expected to be waited on hand and foot.

There was a handsome gilt-framed mirror hanging over the mantelshelf and she stood in front of it to carefully untie the ribbons that held her stylish hat in place. She stared at her reflection. Did she look like a servant? Is that why she had been erroneously sent to the upper floors?

Her hair was a rich, nut-brown with a satisfactory number of curls, her eyes a strange mixture of green and violet. Apart from these two items she thought her appearance unremarkable. She was tall and slender, with just sufficient bosom to distinguish her front from her back.

Freddie, her darling husband who had died in battle, had thought her an incomparable – but then he was biased in her favour. Whether she was attractive or not she was quite certain she didn't look as if she belonged in the servants' hall.

Her ensemble was the height of fashion, had been made by a London modiste, and she doubted that anyone in employment could afford such expensive garments. She removed her travelling cloak and placed it with her bonnet on a convenient side table.

The welcome sound of crockery rattling on a tray heralded the arrival of the much-needed refreshments. Mary was certain that Beth was quite capable of arranging her own repast and did not require any assistance on her part. Her role was that of a friend, here merely to offer support until the girl had found her feet in her new, aristocratic family.

The fact that the duke had not bothered to greet his cousin, but sent his younger brother, confirmed her worst fears. They were not welcome here.

* * *

Aubrey, appalled by his new cousin's lack of manners, couldn't fail to have noticed how lovely she was. He was halfway across the hall when he cursed under his breath. He had failed to bid farewell to Mrs Williams and she must think him as a rag-mannered as her charge.

He turned to remedy this omission but the lady in question was already almost up the grand staircase. He watched her for a moment. His stock became unaccountably tight and an unpleasant heat travelled from his boots to his crown. He was a nincompoop, a buffoon, a veritable greenhorn.

Mrs Williams was no more a companion than he was. How could he have been so blind? She was every inch a lady. Why in God's name had her mother deliberately misled them in her letter?

The housekeeper emerged from the back staircase looking as flustered as he felt. There was no need for him to tell her a dreadful mistake had been made, for she was obviously aware of that fact. She curtsied.

'My lord, Mrs Williams is being moved immediately from the unsuitable accommodation she was given. I'm afraid she is not at all pleased about the mistake. The guest apartment is not ready and she is in the peacock room whilst things are made right for her.'

'Excellent. I shall go and apologise to her immediately. Make sure that Cook is aware Mrs Williams is a guest.'

Anderson curtsied and hurried away. This error was no fault of the staff. In fact, the only person to be blamed for it was Mrs Cassidy. Explaining this to her already angry daughter wasn't a task he would relish. It was a damnable nuisance that Beau had been called urgently to London, as he would have dealt with the matter with more assurance and dignity than himself.

As he approached, the door to the smaller drawing room opened and two parlourmaids appeared carrying laden trays. 'Here, give one to me. I'll take it in.'

The girl looked somewhat surprised by his unusual request but passed it over without comment. The door was ajar so he used his shoulder to push it open and stepped in, closely followed by the other girl.

Mrs Williams had her back to him. 'Put it on the sideboard. I shall ring if I require anything else.'

He did as she instructed before replying. 'You seem to have both coffee and chocolate – which shall I pour for you?'

She reacted as if he had poked her with a sharp stick. 'Good heavens! I'd no idea that this place is so short of staff, Lord Aubrey, that you are reduced to carrying trays yourself.'

He couldn't prevent his smile. 'I've come to grovel, ma'am, for consigning you to the upper regions of the house instead of giving you your rightful place.'

Her eyes twinkled but her lips remained firm. 'I should prefer coffee, sir, if you would be so kind as to pour me some. As you are determined to act as my maidservant, I would also like a little of whatever is on the other tray.' She walked gracefully to the table positioned in front of the window and took one of the chairs beside it.

He poured not one, but two cups of coffee and carried both across. 'I hope you will permit me to join you, Mrs Williams. I don't normally eat now but the appetising aromas made me realise how long it is since I broke my fast.'

She nodded regally and pointed to the place at the other side of the table. 'I shall be glad of the company, my lord. However, I warn you that we might be joined by Miss Freemantle and all sensible conversation will then be impossible.'

'Then we must endeavour to become acquainted before she arrives.' He returned from the sideboard with two full plates and then made a third journey to collect the necessary cutlery and napkins. By the time he had finished she was having difficulty hiding her smile.

He winked at her and this was her undoing. She laughed out loud and, instead of being shocked by such unladylike behaviour, the delightful sound made him join in.

He flicked aside his coat-tails and sat down. 'Whilst we are on good terms, can I explain to you how this error occurred?'

When she heard, instead of being upset or shocked, she laughed again. 'Mama did not mean to have me banished to the servants' quarters – she has never been good with words. Much as I love Beth, she has run my mother ragged these past few years. I always thought it a bad idea to tell the girl how wealthy she was – far better if she had grown up believing she was of modest means.'

'I understand that my cousin is seventeen years of age. Forgive me for saying so, but her behaviour is that of someone considerably younger. Is she perhaps more beautiful than she is intelligent?'

'One might suppose so, indeed. But do not be fooled, sir, she is as bright as she is pretty. What she lacks is maturity and self-discipline. She has been spoilt, petted and granted every wish that money can buy ever since she was out of leading strings. I sincerely hope that the duke can take her in hand before she ruins her good name.'

He dropped his fork with a clatter. 'Has she already shown an inclination to become embroiled with unsuitable gentlemen?'

'I must warn you, my lord, that I fear she has already decided to set her cap at you or your brother. I think the sooner we have her in London and away from here the better. Once she is surrounded by attractive young gentlemen, attending events every evening, she will forget about her plans to ensnare a Sheldon for herself.'

'The chit is in for a rude awakening if she attempts to entrap my brother. He is as likely to put her over his knee as fall for her wiles.' He joined her at the table, finding he was enjoying this extraordinary conversation.

'And what about you, Lord Aubrey? Are you able to withstand her beauty?'

'I admit that the girl is a diamond of the first water, but I could never become entangled with someone as young and silly as my new cousin.' He nodded and smiled at his companion. 'In fact, Mrs Williams, I'm not on the marriage mart. I intend to follow my older brother's example and wait until I am nearer my thirtieth birthday than my twentieth.'

She looked at him speculatively. 'Before I approached the duke I did considerable research into your family. I was not about to send Beth into a rackety lot, if that's what you proved to be.'

She paused as if expecting him to interrupt but he gestured that she should continue. 'I believe that Lord Sheldon married money to improve the family coffers. If your pockets were still to let, then I would have been reluctant to bring her here.'

Aubrey had heard quite enough of this impertinence. He carefully replaced his cutlery and stood up so he was towering over her. 'Madam, I find your comments insolent. You are a guest here and would do well to remember it.'

Instead of apologising she sprung to her feet. Her expression was as frosty as his. 'I speak my mind, sir, and have no intention of begging your pardon for doing so. You are not head of this household and I shall remain here until asked to leave by the duke himself.'

How things might have ended he'd no idea as at that moment Cousin Elizabeth burst into the room. She seemed quite unaware of the tension crackling in the air and rushed across to throw her arms around his neck. 'Cousin Aubrey, I cannot tell you how glad I am to meet you.'

This unexpected attack caused him to stagger backwards and if it wasn't for the intervention of Mrs Williams both he and the girl would have ended in an undignified heap on the carpet.

'Beth, I am shocked by your appalling lack of manners. You will curtsy to his lordship and beg his pardon.'

Aubrey had put a safe distance between himself and the girl, not sure she wouldn't launch herself at him a second time.

'I am sorry for embracing you, Cousin Aubrey.' The girl dipped in a deep curtsy and then quite spoilt the moment by peeping out at him through her long lashes.

He was unable to resist her smile and found himself responding. He bowed. 'Your apology is accepted. But I warn you not to do the same with my brother when you meet him – he would not be so ready to forgive such a breach of etiquette.'

She nodded. 'I think it unlikely that I should wish to embrace him anyway, my lord, as he is an old gentleman – not someone young and attractive like yourself.'

He was at a loss to know how to answer this outrageous statement and made the error of looking at Mrs Williams. She was watching the interchange with obvious amusement.

'Cousin Elizabeth, if you wish me to escort you about Town then you would do well to curb your tongue. Such comments would not go down well in society drawing rooms and you would find yourself ostracised.'

He turned his attention to Mrs Williams. 'No doubt you will expect me to organise vouchers for Almack's. Unless I have your word that your charge will behave with propriety and not bring scandal to our good name, I think it best if she returns to Somerset.'

The girl's happy smile faded, to be replaced by one of anguish. She ran to her companion and clutched at her hands. 'Please, dearest Mary, tell him I will behave. I could not bear to go back to Somerset. I do so wish to see the sights, ride in the park in the afternoon, and eat an ice cream at Gunter's.'

Yet again he was nonplussed by this response.

'I cannot tell him that, sweetheart. It is you who must assure him you will behave like the other young ladies, and not embarrass the family to which you now belong.'

3

Mary kept her arm around the shivering girl and turned to face the young man she had underestimated. He was obviously some years younger than herself and she had thought it would be easy to influence him. However, he was a force to be reckoned with and she must follow her own advice and bite her tongue before she spoke in future.

'Lord Aubrey, it is I who must apologise for speaking so bluntly. Forgive me – I fear the length of the journey has quite overcome my common sense.'

Beth glanced at her in bewilderment and well she might – travelling across England was as nothing compared to travelling on the Continent during a war.

Fortunately, his lordship found nothing untoward in her statement and his frigid expression relaxed a little. 'The matter is forgotten, ma'am. I shall leave you to your refreshments. I suggest that you both dine upstairs tonight and we can start afresh in the morning.'

He strolled out, every inch an aristocrat. The duke would, no doubt, be even more formidable and intractable. If both she and

Beth were not more circumspect in their behaviour they could find themselves returning to Somerset.

'Beth, I believe that we are both a little out of our depth here. We must tread more carefully if we don't want to be denied the treat of a London Season. Now, sit down and I shall bring you something to eat.'

The girl sniffed. 'I wanted to put on one of my new evening gowns tonight and now I shall not be able to do so.'

'Never mind, you can save it for when his grace is here. It's quite possible he will invite Lord Carshalton and Lady Madeline to meet you. Which reminds me, I wonder why Lady Giselle has not appeared?'

Beth's disappointment was forgotten. 'I know the answer to that. She broke her leg a few weeks ago and is still not able to come down. Does that mean she won't come to London?'

'As we are not going until April she has ample time to get on her feet. It will be much more enjoyable attending all the parties if your cousin is there too. I'm sure we can pay her a visit tomorrow.'

'Why can't we go up now? She must be eager to meet me and be bored to distraction after so long closeted in her apartment.'

Mary was about to veto this suggestion but then reconsidered. 'We shall finish this, then I must remove my boots and tidy myself. I should also like to see your rooms. After that we will go in search of your cousin.'

'Anna said that you are in a different wing to me – I don't like to think of you so far away.'

'I've no idea how your maid is privy to this information – but she is correct. We shall investigate each other's apartments and then will both know how to find one another.'

Half an hour later they were suitably attired and ready to venture out again. Despite his curmudgeonly behaviour, Lord Aubrey had arranged for a helpful footman to wait outside to conduct them wherever they wanted. She spoke to the one designated to assist Beth.

'We wish to visit Lady Giselle. Would you enquire if she is receiving this afternoon?'

He bowed and walked to the other end of the spacious passageway and knocked on a door. Mary hastily tugged her charge back into the room. It would not do to be seen lurking in the corridor.

'It's possible she is resting and doesn't want to see us. I don't want any nonsense from you if that's the case.'

The footman tapped on the door before Beth could answer. Mary just had time to grab the girl's arm before she rushed over to answer the summons herself.

'Come in,' Mary called.

'Lady Giselle is receiving and would be pleased for you to visit, ma'am.'

* * *

The two girls became bosom bows immediately. Mary left them chattering excitedly about the forthcoming Season and the necessity to replenish their already overstocked wardrobes. Lady Giselle was walking quite well with only the slightest limp visible.

They were to eat their supper together, which meant she had an entire evening to herself. She would spend it writing in her journal – she had kept one since she was first able to write to legibly. Reading this was her solace and her joy, as it kept the memory of her beloved husband alive.

Although she had never attended a Season herself, she was well aware that the main events didn't begin until April at the earliest – many of the most prestigious families didn't arrive in

Town until the end of that month. If there was to be a ball for the two girls, then matters must be put in hand immediately. It was imperative invitations were sent out as soon as possible so that the event didn't clash with another.

There was only one way to set things in motion and that involved speaking to the objectionable young man and discovering exactly what the family intended to do. It was possible, of course, that there was a married relative already designated to take control. She sincerely hoped that was the case, as then she could return to Suffolk. Not to rejoin her mother, but to her own estate to which she should have gone when she was widowed three years ago.

There was no footman outside her sitting room door. Presumably he thought she was intending to remain in her rooms until the morning. She wasn't sure when they dined here, but even if they kept country hours and ate at five o'clock, his lordship would not have gone up to change just yet.

She glanced over the balustrade in the gallery but couldn't see any servants lurking about. She would go down and find a bell to ring – with luck she should be able to retrace her steps to the pretty drawing room she'd used earlier.

* * *

Aubrey felt he had acquitted himself dismally. Beau expected him to take charge of things in his absence and he was making a sad mull of it. His lips twitched. Perhaps he was being unduly hard on himself as he rather thought his brother might have been even more incensed than he by Mrs Williams' remarks.

He flopped onto a chair in front of the fire in Beau's study and picked up a journal that had arrived that morning. He was engrossed in an interesting article about a forthcoming horse race when he was disturbed by a soft tap on the door.

Without looking up he bid whoever it was to come in, expecting it to be a servant with a message.

'I apologise for disturbing you, my lord, but I must speak to you most urgently.'

He dropped his paper and sprung to his feet. What the devil was she doing here?

'Mrs Williams, why have you come here?' This was hardly a polite greeting.

'I have left your cousin and your sister discussing their come-out. I accompanied Beth to act as her chaperone and to organise her schedule. I wish to know if you will need me to make these arrangements.'

'You had better come in and sit down, ma'am; we can hardly discuss this with you hovering in the doorway like that.' He strode across the room and took his position behind the huge leather-topped desk, leaving her to take the uncomfortable chair that faced it.

She seemed unbothered by his abruptness and settled herself on the chair before staring him straight in the eye. 'The girls are already talking about their ball – have things been put in hand for this?'

Why was she asking him this question? Until a few days ago not even he had known there was to be a ball. 'I can say with the utmost certainty, Mrs Williams, that nothing has been put in hand. I know nothing of such matters. Are you suggesting this should be done before we leave for Town?'

Her eyes widened slightly; he was certain she was grinding her teeth. What could he have done to upset her this time?

'Lord Aubrey, invitations must be sent out in the next couple of days if we are to have the date for ourselves. I am assuming from your blank expression that nothing at all has been done to make the Season a success for Beth and Lady Giselle.'

She didn't wait for him to respond but continued blithely, presumably unaware that he was having difficulty holding on to his temper.

'Does his grace have a secretary?'

He nodded but felt it better to remain silent rather than say what he was thinking.

'That is good news indeed. I shall work with him and we will have things set in motion in no time. What is the gentleman's name?'

'My brother's man of business is Mr Carstairs and he has a young man, whose name escapes me, working with him.'

'All the expenses involved, including the cost of the girls' wardrobes, will be met by the Freemantle estate. Do not poker up at me, sir, as if I had no right to know these things. Mr Gregson, who has dealt with Beth's affairs since her birth, has already set aside an extravagant sum with which to pay these expenses.'

She smiled at him as if he was an errant schoolboy and it was his turn to clench his jaw.

'There's no need to feel inadequate, sir; one cannot expect a young stripling like yourself to be *au fait* with what is needed in the circumstances.'

This last remark was the outside of enough. He surged to his feet, braced his hands on the desk and leaned across so he was less than a yard from her.

'Yet again, madam, you forget to whom you speak. I am a Sheldon. You are a nobody. You will not be accompanying my cousin to London and neither will you be acting in the role of chaperone. A more suitable person will be found.'

She didn't look at all put out by his tirade. She shook her head slightly and half-smiled. 'In which case, sir, I'm even more delighted. However, as I believe I mentioned earlier, I shall remain here until I have spoken to the head of the household in person and not one of his younger siblings.'

Before he could respond with a suitably pithy reply she was out of the door. He picked up a ledger and hurled it after. It struck the door with a satisfying crash when it was half closed. The sound of her laughter only added to his fury.

Beau would be horrified when he heard of the altercation. His brother never had to raise his voice to make his point. The mere lift of an eyebrow or the straightening of a lip was enough to send his opponents scurrying for cover.

The wretched woman was correct to point out that arrangements for any big event should be in hand by now. He'd attended several of these prestigious balls and everything from the white soup to the flower arrangements had been set in motion by someone similar to her.

When Beau had said he must go to London in his stead, he hadn't understood exactly what that would mean. He'd imagined it would just require him to saunter about with a pretty girl on his arm whilst keeping a careful eye out for fortune hunters and other undesirables.

He was damned if he was going to waste the next four months obliged to spend time with someone whom he cordially disliked. She made him feel like a nincompoop and this was not a comfortable feeling.

* * *

The duke was conspicuous by his absence, which meant that Mary had been left with a difficult choice. Either she continued to eat her supper alone in her rooms or she sat with the objectionable Lord Aubrey. She decided to remain in solitary splendour until the missing aristocrat deigned to return home.

However, she was not idle in the interim. Despite his lordship's incivility she sent for Gregson and Carstairs the next morning and set things in motion. Both of these astute men of business approved of her taking control.

'I shall have invitations sent out to the appropriate families, Mrs Williams,' Carstairs said. 'Do you wish me to engage extra staff for that evening?'

'I think that is best left to the butler. He will know where to find the most suitable candidates for temporary employment. Lady Giselle and Miss Freemantle will need gowns – whilst you are in London would you arrange for whoever takes care of these matters for this family to come down with samples and fashion plates?'

He nodded. 'I think that is everything, ma'am. Will Miss Freemantle wish to ride?'

'She will not, thank you, as she has no liking for the pastime. I should like a spirited mount to be available for myself. Gregson will purchase one for me as he knows exactly what I prefer.'

The two men were to work in tandem and appeared to be satisfied with this arrangement. The young man who acted as Carstairs' secretary, Culley, would remain behind to convey any messages she might have.

She refused to be cooped up inside a moment longer but could hardly demand a horse to ride when things were so touchy between her and the man supposedly in charge of the household. She must make do with brisk walks around the gardens until his grace returned.

Although Lady Giselle continued to improve she and Beth preferred to eat upstairs. She scarcely saw her charge and when she did she was pleasantly surprised at the change in her behaviour and appearance. The gowns she had declared were her favourites, the ones with a surfeit of rouleau and ribbons, were now abandoned for unadorned versions that Mary had not known she owned.

When she joined them three days after their arrival, Beth greeted her with enthusiasm.

'Mary, Giselle and I have decided that we would like our gowns to be similar. When is the modiste coming to take our measurements and show us the patterns?'

'She should be here sometime today, my dear. I must say you do look alike – you could be mistaken for sisters rather than cousins. I know your cousin is dark and you are fair, but in every other respect you are very similar.'

'Giselle has loaned me some of her gowns until I can have a fresh wardrobe made up.' Beth smiled. 'You did tell me I was making a mistake to order gowns with so much decoration and I should have listened to you.'

'I was aware that you look far more elegant and grown-up. Thank you, Lady Giselle...'

The girl interrupted. 'Please, won't you call me Giselle? You are part of the family too.'

'I'm not sure that would be a good idea, perhaps we should wait until his grace returns and ask his opinion?'

'We all address each other by our given names when here. I'm sure he will agree that such formality should be abandoned forthwith.'

'In which case, Giselle, you must call me Mary as Beth does.'

The matter settled, the conversation turned to the absence of the duke. 'It's not like my brother to be away so long without sending word. I cannot think what is detaining him. I wish to surprise him by coming down to dinner.'

'One would think that Carstairs would be cognisant of his

whereabouts – but he too is unable to locate him. Can I prevail on you girls to come down this evening, as I am heartily sick of eating on my own in my apartment?'

They were shocked by her admission and immediately agreed they would dine downstairs that evening.

'I have two maids busy removing the unnecessary adornment from my gowns, Mary, and have something that I'm sure you will agree is now quite delightful.'

'Will you send word to the kitchen, Giselle?'

'I shall send someone down immediately. Peebles will be pleased to be able to have dinner served. Aubrey has also been eating in his rooms these past few nights.'

* * *

Mary paid particular attention to her ensemble that evening. Jessie stepped back to admire her work. 'Russet is perfect with your colouring, madam. Are you going to wear the emeralds that match your eyes?'

'I believe that I will do so. After all, I am dining in one of the grandest houses in the country and wish to look my best. Not the tiara – just the ear bobs and necklace.'

The parure had been a gift from her husband on their wedding and had been in his family for generations. She might not have a title, but she believed herself to be the equal of any aristocrat she might happen to meet.

Her inelegant snort of laughter at this absurd thought caused her maid to drop the necklace. Mary could hardly share her thoughts. She was more than a match for Lord Aubrey. After all, had she not dined with heads of state, dukes and duchesses when with Freddie? As he had been the colonel of his regiment, he had been expected to attend all the banquets and state dinners.

She was roused from her reverie by the arrival of the girls. 'You look lovely, Mary. I don't believe I've seen that gown before,' Beth said.

'As do you, my love. Damask rose is perfect on you. Giselle, that is an unusual shade of blue – I like it very well.'

'Poor Aubrey will be quite outshone by us tonight. I cannot wait to see his face when he views us in our evening elegance.'

The girls linked arms and walked ahead chattering gaily. Beth had been sadly starved of acquaintances of her own age and Mary was beginning to think her wild behaviour was a direct result of not having suitable friends of her own.

She was tempted to address the irascible lord by his first name just to see his reaction but thought he would have more than enough to cope with without adding to his discomfiture by teasing him.

4

Aubrey was about to leave his apartment when Beau strolled in. 'Good God! When did you get back? I can't tell you how glad I am to see you.'

'I apologise for my absence, little brother, but it was unavoidable. I'm only here to meet our cousin and then have to depart for our estates in Northumberland. I'm afraid you're going to have to act in my stead, however much you dislike the idea.'

'Have you met Elizabeth or Mrs Williams? The former is a practised flirt and the latter thoroughly objectionable. I've no wish to spend time with either of them here, or in London.'

'It's not like you to be so scathing in your opinions about people you've only just met. Unfortunately, whatever you feel about the matter, you have no choice.' Beau patted him on the shoulder. 'I give you my word that if they are as impossible as you imply they will return post-haste from whence they came.'

'Then I am satisfied. You will see at once that neither of them will do. Our cousin dresses in gowns best suited to a circus tent and Mrs Williams... well I cannot recall what she wears but it certainly isn't elegant.'

It was the custom for the family to gather in the drawing room before going through to dine; tonight was to be no exception. The double doors were open and he and Beau took their usual places in front of the fire.

From where he was positioned, Aubrey couldn't see the ladies arriving but he could hear them – at least he could hear his sister and cousin chattering together.

'Giselle, sweetheart, I can't tell you how pleased I am to see you downstairs.' Beau rushed forward to greet the new arrivals. Aubrey waited for him to be bombarded with sycophantic chatter but heard nothing from his cousin.

'Your grace, I am Mrs Williams. Allow me to introduce you to your cousin, Miss Elizabeth Freemantle.'

Aubrey moved so he could watch this farce unfold. His eyes widened and he ran his finger around his neckcloth, which had become unaccountably tight. How had this metamorphosis taken place in so short a time? Curtsying demurely to his brother was the most beautiful girl he'd ever set eyes on. Her hair was arranged in the same manner as his sister, and her evening gown was stunning.

If she was transformed then her companion was even more so. Standing composed and elegant was the woman he had dismissed as plain. She was wearing an exquisite emerald necklace, which must have cost a king's ransom. Even he recognised her gown as being cut by an expert.

His brother took the hands of his cousin. 'I'm delighted to have you here, my dear. I can see that you have been a wonderful influence on my sister already.' He turned to Mrs Williams. 'I hesitate to ask, ma'am, but were you by any chance married to Colonel Frederick Williams?'

Her face was transformed by her smile. 'I was indeed, your grace. Did you know my husband?'

'I had the pleasure of meeting him at a state banquet. My brother, Lord Sheldon, served under him. He and his wife, as well as my sister and her new husband, should be arriving at any moment. They are eager to meet you both. I don't think that Bennett has realised who you are.'

He was interrupted as his brother and his wife walked in, having overheard his comment.

'I can't believe it. I met with Lord Sheldon often and liked him very well. My husband was certain he would replace him as colonel.' Her radiant smile slipped a little. 'Freddie was killed shortly after your brother resigned his commission.'

'Mary, my dear, I should have made the connection.' Bennett held out his arms and to Aubrey's astonishment she rushed in to be embraced like a sister.

'Bennett, as you didn't use your title when serving, I had no idea you were part of this prestigious family. How different things might have been if we had ever talked of our families.' She stepped away. 'Beth could have grown up here surrounded by her cousins.'

He introduced her to Grace, Madeline and Carshalton, who had just arrived. Aubrey was forced to admit that maybe he had been hasty in his judgement. Beth was behaving impeccably and Mrs Williams was as at ease with his family as someone born to the position.

His intention was to eat a large slice of humble pie and put matters right between them, but Peebles announced that dinner was served and the opportunity was lost. Naturally she sat next to Bennett and he took his place next to Beau.

The conversation around the table was lively and he watched Beth to see if she would take wine when it was offered. Giselle shook her head slightly and immediately the girl did likewise.

'Aubrey, I'm at a loss to see why you have taken a dislike to either of these new arrivals. I find Mrs Williams intelligent, elegant and a welcome member to this select group. Whatever Beth might have been when she arrived, our sister has worked wonders and the girl is now as charming as she is beautiful.'

Aubrey smiled ruefully. 'I agree with everything you say, brother. I think I shall manage perfectly well in London escorting the girls to their various parties. Mrs Williams said that we should have matters in hand for the ball.'

'Gregson explained that he was tasked with sending out the invitations. You can leave everything in the capable hands of Mrs Williams. All you have to do, little brother, is see that neither of the girls is pursued by undesirables. Although Giselle has the title and a sizeable dowry, Beth will be equally popular. The fact that both of them are lovely girls will only add to your problems.'

'I shall enlist the help of Mrs Williams. Between us we will keep them safe. Do you expect our sister to become engaged?'

'God's teeth! I hope not – I don't wish to lose her so soon.' He frowned and then relaxed. 'However, she is nineteen years of age – many young ladies are already married by then. I should not stand in her way if she met the man of her dreams, but this place will be too quiet without her.'

The remainder of the evening was spent in convivial conversation, a hand or two of piquet, and then the party dispersed. Aubrey rather thought that he might well require his brother to help out with the girls before the Season was over. Beau was leaving at first light for Northumbria and expected to be there for several weeks but gave his word he would join them in London as soon as he could.

* * *

The next few weeks were gone in a rush of mantua-makers, milliners and family gatherings. Mary was now riding out every morning and was feeling all the better for the exercise. The girls were so eager to begin their visit to Town that she was persuaded to leave the first week of April.

The duke had made it perfectly clear she was in charge of this operation and that his brother was merely there to fend off unwanted suitors. The young man was personable and appeared reasonably intelligent, but he was several years her junior and, however hard she tried, she couldn't consider him as an equal.

Fortunately, Beth was no longer setting her cap at him and behaving as if she had been part of the family for months rather than weeks. The duke was still absent but had written to say he hoped to have concluded his business before the date of the ball – this gave him more than a month.

His lordship was also away from Silchester. He had not thought fit to inform her of his whereabouts, or the length of his visit, therefore she felt no qualms about bringing forward the date of their departure by two weeks.

The luggage left first thing in the morning, with the three maids, and should arrive in Grosvenor Square with ample time to ensure their trunks were unpacked and everything was ready for their arrival.

'It is but a short distance to London, Beth, so we should be there without the necessity of stopping for refreshments. The weather is clement and the journey should be pleasant,' Mary said as she settled onto the squabs on the opposite side to the two girls.

'After the tiresome journey from Somerset, a few hours are a mere bagatelle. I wonder how many more acceptances we have received for our ball.'

'At the last count all but a handful had replied in the affirmative. I imagine there will be dozens of invitations to other events waiting to be examined.' The girls did not seem unduly bothered by her statement.

'I'm more interested in seeing our evening gowns, and they will not be ready until next week. Thank goodness we have all our day clothes so can visit the sights immediately,' Giselle said, and Beth agreed.

* * *

The Silchester house was as impressive as their country estate. It was set back from the road a satisfactory distance and had handsome iron gates to welcome them in. The carriage, naturally, could not go through these gates as there would be no room for it to turn in front of the house. Horses and vehicles continued and entered through an archway to access the rear of the property.

'The outrider has alerted the staff, girls, and the footmen are already on their way to let down the steps and escort us inside. They will bring your belongings – there's no need to carry anything but your reticules.'

As they walked in there was a rumble of thunder and the first few spots of rain began to fall. 'Pick up your skirts; we must make a dash for it.' Mary led the way and they reached the shelter of the porch just as the heavens opened.

The footmen were not so lucky. 'They should have brought umbrellas with them. I should not have been best pleased if my new bonnet had been ruined by this downpour,' Beth said.

Before Mary could chide her for her comment, her friend remonstrated gently. 'Think of the poor young men getting drenched on our behalf – they don't have a wardrobe full of fresh clothes to change into as we do.'

Beth wasn't listening as she had walked into the entrance hall and was gazing in wonder at the splendour of it all. 'This is a very handsome house, Giselle. I believe I shall be very happy here.'

Mary was ushered to a suitably grand apartment on the family side of the house and not in the guest wing. The girls were to share – this was their choice not from necessity. Jessie greeted her with a curtsy.

'I have hot water here, ma'am, and a fresh ensemble if you would care to change.'

'I shall wash my face and hands, but there is no need to change. This gown has come to no harm on the journey.' She removed her bonnet and the pretty blue spencer that matched the forget-me-nots woven into the fabric of her new gown.

When she was done she explored her surroundings and was delighted to find the windows of her sitting room overlooked a charming garden, which was far larger than she had expected in a town house. There was a loud knock on her door and before she could answer the girls rushed in.

'May we go downstairs and look at the invitations, Mary? Do you think there might be something for this evening?' Beth asked.

'As we weren't expected to be here until the end of the month I should very much doubt it. I think it will be far better to have time to settle in and explore the city before we are obliged to attend parties every night. Once this begins we will not find our beds until the small hours and it's unlikely there will be any time or inclination for sightseeing.'

Giselle nodded. 'I haven't been to London for an age. The last time I was here I was still in the schoolroom and not allowed to venture out on my own.'

'And neither will you be this time, my dear. A young lady does not go out on her own – it is not done and it certainly isn't safe for either of you. I shall accompany you at all times.'

'That will be quite different than it was before. Last time I still had a governess and she was not at all jolly.'

'We will receive morning calls or return them most afternoons so we must make the most of our leisure time whilst we still have it.'

* * *

Aubrey returned to Silchester Court after spending a pleasant couple of days with a crony who had recently purchased a small stud and wanted his opinion. Whilst away he had decided to make his peace with Mrs Williams, as it would be uncomfortable for both of them if they were at odds when they went to London.

He hadn't taken his valet with him for so short a stay and his man had been decidedly disgruntled by this omission.

'I hope you enjoyed your respite from taking care of me, Wells. Has anything of import transpired in my absence?' This was a casual question and he didn't expect to receive an answer in the affirmative.

'Lady Giselle, Miss Freemantle and Mrs Williams left for London yesterday. Do you wish me to pack your trunks, my lord?'

'It's too late to depart today but we shall leave at first light. We shall travel in my curricle so will only be able to take a small box. Arrange for the remainder of my luggage to follow as soon as may be.'

He thought he had concealed his fury admirably. He had no wish for gossip from below stairs to follow him to Town.

What had possessed the woman to leave so suddenly? She had no authority to remove his sister and cousin from his protection. Just as he was becoming resigned to spending time with her she had angered him again.

Although he searched he found no note left for him

explaining why she had left before the agreed date. He dined in his rooms and was in a foul temper when he retired, having drunk far more brandy than was good for him.

As he was drifting off to sleep he saw an image of Beth in his head. She was startlingly lovely, lively and now prettily behaved. Despite his reservations about her companion he had to admit he was glad his cousin had come to join the family. Was it possible he was interested in her for himself? Was he ready to step into parson's mousetrap with such a tempting morsel on offer?

He awoke the next morning with a mouth as dry as sand and a head that rang like a bell. He'd forego breakfast – his stomach was roiling from last night's excesses – and he and his valet were on their way before the stable clock struck six.

Being a notable whipster, Aubrey was confident he could cover the distance to London in a couple of hours and arrive in Grosvenor Square before the escapees had time to gallivant to Hatchards, or some other such place.

The roads were relatively free of traffic and even when he reached the outskirts of the city he only had to negotiate a few diligences and carts on his way to his destination. He turned the curricle expertly under the arch and drew his matched bays to a smart halt.

He tossed his whip, hat, and gloves to his valet and walked briskly to the side door. He had not sent word ahead that he was arriving this morning but the house was so efficiently run that his early appearance would not throw the staff into any sort of panic.

His smile was grim as he entered. The only person he wished to panic was Mrs Williams. He had rehearsed what he intended to say on the drive and was certain by the time he'd finished she would be in no doubt as to his opinion on the matter.

Breakfast would not be served for another hour, so he had sufficient time to restore his appearance and be downstairs before she arrived. Should he send for her – insist that she met him in the study – or surprise her when she came in to break her fast?

He paced the study trying to make a decision. He didn't wish to upset the girls so perhaps it would be better to speak to Mrs Williams alone. He would write her a note and demand that she attend him immediately.

He read the note again:

Mrs Williams

I am waiting in the study to speak to you. You will attend me there immediately.

Yes, that would do. She would be in no doubt that he was angry at her desertion. In Beau's absence he was the man of the house and the sooner she understood that the better they would deal together.

He had been told that Mrs Williams was up, so he expected her to arrive within fifteen minutes of his letter being sent. After kicking his heels for half an hour he was incensed – he was damned if he was going to wait for her a moment longer. He would go to her apartment himself.

5

As always Mary was in the stable yard before anyone in the household was awake, apart from the servants. The horse Gregson had bought her, a large dappled grey gelding, greeted her affectionately, leaving a trail of slobber down her once immaculate riding habit. His behaviour was relaxed with her and the stable boys, but he wouldn't let an adult male anywhere near him.

A groom accompanied her on her ride but remained respectfully behind her and in no way interfered with her enjoyment. The park was no more than a fifteen-minute jog from the house and once she was there she could let her mount stretch his legs.

The three mornings she had been out at this time she had met no other riders so was able to push Red into a gallop without fear of being seen by anyone who mattered. An hour later she returned to the stables ready to face the day.

The prestigious dressmaker had now delivered the remainder of their wardrobes and the girls were eager to accept their first invitation now they had the requisite garments. Reluctantly she had agreed they could go to an informal supper party at Lord and

Lady Bridport's house, which was the other side of the square. The party began at seven o'clock and was stated to finish by midnight. This seemed an innocuous enough event and would be ideal to introduce her charges into the *ton*.

The house was now alive, the footmen busy about their morning duties and the butler – a supercilious gentleman – appeared to smirk as she walked past. Surely not? She must have imagined it.

Her sitting room door was ajar and she was certain she had left it closed. She hurried forward, curious to know who might have gone in without her permission. She was shocked to find her nemesis haranguing her maid for information as to her whereabouts.

'Lord Aubrey – might I enquire what you are doing in my private quarters?' Her disapproval dripped from every word.

He turned, his eyes hard and his face looking older than his years. For a moment she was concerned but then reminded herself she had dealt with far more formidable gentlemen in the past.

'You have been riding—'

She interrupted him. 'How very observant of you, sir. A less intelligent gentleman might not have noticed I am wearing my habit.' She tapped her foot and raised an enquiring eyebrow, which perhaps wasn't the most sensible of responses.

In two strides he was no more than an arm's length from her. 'I wish to speak to you—'

Again, she stopped him in mid-sentence. 'Certainly, my lord, but you will not do so in my chambers. Kindly remove yourself. I shall join you shortly and you will have my full attention then.' She waved a hand in dismissal, ignored his fulminating stare, and sailed past him into the safety of her bedroom.

She leaned against the closed door, holding her breath,

thinking for an awful moment he might come after her. After a few moments she heard him leave and regretted her behaviour.

He should not have come into her apartment, but she should have been more accommodating. Indeed, she had inflamed the situation horribly and had no one to blame but herself. She would change quickly and go and find him. She must beg his pardon and hope he might forgive her appalling lapse of manners.

After all she had taken the girls away without his permission and the duke had left them in Lord Aubrey's charge. She stripped and completed her ablutions in rapid time. She scarcely noticed the gown she stepped into as she was more concerned in making amends.

'Madam, I forgot, this note came up for you whilst you were out riding.'

Jessie handed the folded rectangle to her and Mary opened it. She read the contents and her eyes narrowed. So that was what he was doing up here – he had come to find her because she had supposedly ignored his rude summons.

How dare he order her about as if she were his lackey? All desire to apologise vanished. She set off determined to let this arrogant young man know exactly what she thought of him. He might be the brother of a duke but that didn't give him the right to run roughshod over her.

Now she understood the sly smile from the butler. He too would get his comeuppance – but one thing at a time. She knew the whereabouts of the study and stalked down the spacious passageway, parade-ground stiff. Her eyes were alight at the prospect of a battle. There was nothing she liked better than routing an opponent. Her life had been dull since she had returned home a widow three years ago. She sorely missed the excitement of being with the regiment – she missed dearest Freddie as well, of course.

If her quarry was not to be found in his study she would go in and wait for him. She was sure her every move was scrutinised by the vigilant staff and he would soon hear that she had invaded his private sanctum. Her lips twitched. Well – strictly speaking the study was the domain of the Duke of Silchester but in his absence she supposed his youngest brother could claim it as his own.

The door was closed. She rapped loudly and waited to be snarled at. When she received no reply she knocked a little louder. Again – nothing. She opened the door and marched in, expecting the room to be unoccupied. His lordship was standing with his back to the door and didn't turn.

'Put the tray down and be about your business.' He obviously believed her to be a servant bringing him his breakfast.

It would have been more sensible to retreat and return when he was in a more responsive mood. However, she was never one to resist a challenge. She moved, soft-footed, until she was no more than a yard behind him. 'I believe you wish to speak to me, my lord.'

His arms shot out and he spun round. She had no time to take evasive action and his flailing fist struck her in the chest and she tumbled backwards.

He was on his knees beside her in a trice. 'Lie still, Mrs Williams. I shall send for assistance. I cannot tell you how sorry I am. I did not realise you were so close beside me. I wouldn't have struck you for the world.'

Mary was perfectly well – just a little winded and regretting her silly prank. 'If you would be kind enough to lend me your arm, sir, I am unhurt and have no need to remain here.'

She was lifted with more speed than dignity to her feet. Then to her chagrin he hoisted her into his arms and carried her to the sofa. 'No, remain where you are. I hear my breakfast arriving; it would not do for the staff to hear us arguing.'

There was a tap on the door and then two footmen sidled in. They placed the trays on the desk and scuttled away. No doubt the fact that she was spreadeagled on the sofa with Lord Aubrey standing over her would be the main topic of conversation below stairs.

'Having floored you, ma'am, may I now fetch you some coffee? Perhaps you would like a snifter of brandy to settle your nerves after such a distressing experience.'

'Coffee would be perfect, my lord, and whatever there is to eat would do splendidly. May I have your permission to sit at that table by the window as I do so hate eating on my lap.'

He chuckled, a surprisingly rich, deep sound that she found quite attractive. 'When you ask my permission to do anything, ma'am, I shall eat your best bonnet.'

She jumped up and winced. Despite her claims that she had been uninjured, she was sure she had a nasty bruise on her chest. Fortunately, he did not see her reaction as she had no wish for him to know he had inadvertently caused her harm.

'I have bread, butter, marmalade and three slices of ham. Is that acceptable or shall I ring for something else to be fetched?'

'It's an eclectic mix, my lord, but I'm sure I shall find it tasty.' She sipped her coffee whilst he piled his own plate and filled his cup. When he was relaxed she could almost like him.

'Could I ask you a favour, sir? Would you please use my given name as it makes me feel like an old lady being constantly referred to as ma'am?'

'I should be delighted to call you Mary.'

She waited for him to suggest that she could also address him informally but he said nothing else and took his place opposite her at the table. Her pleasure in the encounter vanished along with her appetite.

Her cutlery clattered noisily onto her plate and she stood up. 'Please excuse me, my lord, I'm not feeling at all the thing after my fall. I shall leave you to your breakfast.'

Instead of leaping to his feet he merely looked up and smiled. 'Sit down, Mary, and don't be a pea-goose. I should have said that you must call me Aubrey but assumed you would know that without my having to say.'

Feeling decidedly foolish, Mary resumed her place. 'I'm not usually so quick to take offence, but for some reason we appear to set each other on edge.'

'I'm normally the most amiable of fellows. Ask my siblings – they will all be quick to say that Perry and I are nothing like Bennett and Beau.' He grinned and she couldn't help responding in kind. 'By the by, I don't suggest you call the duke by his given name.'

'Good heavens! I might be, as you have so kindly pointed out, a pea-goose but I am not entirely lacking in common sense.'

He gestured towards her uneaten food. 'Please be good enough to consume your breakfast or I shall feel the veriest villain for having put you off your food.'

Although her appetite had now returned she couldn't do justice to the food as swallowing was extremely painful. She sipped her coffee but even that caused some difficulty.

'Tarnation take it! You are in some distress because of me. I am sending for the physician – Dr Adams, he must examine you.'

'Your fist hit me in the chest and has caused some bruising, which is making it painful to eat or drink. I'm certain there is nothing more serious. I should not be able to breathe comfortably if I had broken anything.'

He reached out and covered her hands with his. 'I shall never forgive myself for injuring you. Please remain where you are whilst I ring for a footman to fetch the doctor.'

'Aubrey, it was not your fault. If I hadn't been acting like a silly schoolgirl it wouldn't have happened. I do not blame you, so you must not blame yourself.'

Gently she removed her hands not wishing to prolong the unnecessary contact. 'If you will not be sanguine unless I'm examined by your physician, then so be it. I shall return to my apartment and he must see me there.'

This time when she got to her feet he was up quicker than she was. 'By the way, I've promised to take the girls across the square to an informal supper party at the home of one of your neighbours. No, don't poker up at me, sir; I have no intention of letting them down. It would make the evening more enjoyable for the girls if you would accompany them as well.'

'I shall do so with pleasure. At what time must I report for duty?'

'The invitation states we should be there by seven o'clock so I would say at a quarter to the hour would be perfect.'

For the first time since they'd met they parted on good terms and Mary thought that possibly the accident might prove to have been a turning point in their relationship. This would make the next few weeks so much easier to deal with. Promenading around dozens of routs, soirées and balls was not something she relished; she would much prefer to be in the country. No, that was incorrect; she would rather be following the drum with her darling Freddie, or indeed, anyone at all. Life as a civilian was not to her taste.

* * *

Aubrey was still hungry after devouring the food on the tray – maybe sharing it with Mary hadn't been such a good idea after all. The small dining room, where breakfast was served, was occupied by the girls.

'Good morning, Beth, Giselle. Are you enjoying your social life in London?'

They were heaping their plates with various delicacies and didn't pause to curtsy, but both replied in the affirmative. 'Mary was worried you would be cross that we had left without you, but I told her she had nothing to worry about on that score,' his sister said blithely.

'We are the best of friends, sweetheart, and I'm looking forward to accompanying you to the party across the square this evening.'

'Do you think there will be dancing?' Beth asked eagerly.

'I have no idea, but sometimes they roll back the carpet in the drawing room and someone volunteers to play the piano.'

'I do like to dance, but that's not why I asked. If there is to be dancing then it would be unwise to wear an evening gown with a train of any sort.' She smiled a trifle hesitantly. 'Am I to address you as Cousin Aubrey or have we now dropped the formality?'

'Call me Aubrey, but not when we are in public. What are you doing today?'

The conversation meandered from one subject to another and he was impressed by Beth's knowledge of world events and interest in the war. She wasn't the feather-brained girl he had thought her but an intelligent and lively young lady.

He left them to their own devices and decided to stroll to his club to catch up on the latest *on dits*. Town would be rather thin of company so early in the Season, but there should be enough gentlemen around to make his visit worthwhile.

The responsibility of keeping not one but two beautiful young heiresses safe from predatory fortune hunters was going to be difficult. His club was the best place to hear any scandal and learn the names of possible suitors he should keep away from the girls.

Even so early in the day the place was busy. He handed his beaver and gloves to the doorman, signed the book, and wandered into the main club room.

'Well look who it is! The very cove we were talking about a few moments back.' David Grantham, an old friend from Oxford, greeted him enthusiastically.

'I'm glad to see you. Why was I the topic of conversation?' He joined his friend, and two other fellows he didn't recognise, at their corner. He waved away the flunky who came to take his order.

'Word has it that you have brought this year's most eligible debutantes with you. Sharks are circling already; every rake and ne'er-do-well looking for a wealthy bride is hoping to ensnare one of them.'

'God's teeth! This is exactly the scenario I was hoping to avoid. How in God's name has word got out when they only arrived last week?'

'As soon as invitations were sent for their come-out ball the tabbies began to gossip. It didn't take long for the chatter to spread about Miss Freemantle being the wealthiest, as well as the most beautiful, young lady in Town this year.' Grantham waved vaguely at the other two listening avidly to the conversation. 'Allow me to introduce you to Sir Richard Dunstan and Jonathan Bishop – new acquaintances of mine.'

A flicker of unease made Aubrey look more closely at these two. Grantham was an easy-going sort of fellow, but not famous for his wit or perspicacity.

Sir Richard was above medium height, had hair almost as dark as his own and a friendly expression. Aubrey thought he was probably nearer his thirtieth year than his twentieth. The other fellow, Bishop, looked innocuous enough but his attire was not to his taste. High shirt points that made turning the head impossible, and a violent red and green waistcoat were fashionable amongst some young bucks but Aubrey thought the fashion ridiculous.

'Delighted, my lord; heard a lot about your family,' Dunstan said amiably. Bishop merely nodded and smiled.

'I cannot say the same about yours. Should I know of you?'

'Not at all – I don't move in the same elevated circles as you. My estates are in Cornwall. Bishop is my cousin on an extended visit here from Ireland.'

Satisfied these two were reasonably innocuous, Aubrey relaxed and the conversation turned to horses and politics. As he took his leave, Grantham touched his arm. 'I've not seen Lady Giselle since she was in the schoolroom; I hope you will allow me to dance with her.'

'She must make that decision for herself, but if you do meet at some function or other I shall not stand in her way.'

He was certain that Grantham would be a harmless dance partner. He might appeal to his sister as he was of an athletic build, tall and considered handsome. He was the heir to an earldom, was wealthy enough and she could do a lot worse than choose him as her husband.

* * *

He was suitably attired in his evening rig and eagerly awaiting the arrival of the ladies at the appointed hour. The girls appeared first, dressed in similar fashion – one in yellow, the other in pink. The waists of their gowns sat under their bosoms, and their hair was arranged so a few beguiling ringlets fell on either side of their faces.

Mary could have looked plain in comparison. Her gown was lacking in sparkles and adornment and her hair was arranged more severely. For some reason it was to her his eyes were drawn. She moved with such grace, her head held high. Her remarkable eyes had more than enough sparkle to compensate for the lack of it on her gown.

6

Two footmen had been designated to accompany them across the square. This seemed quite unnecessary to Mary as the weather was fine and the sun still shining. No doubt when they returned in the dark they would be glad of an escort carrying flambeaux.

'Remember, girls, you must be on your best behaviour as this is your first venture into society. I know you have both attended parties and balls in the country, but the rules are stricter here and if you don't wish to tarnish your reputation, you will abide by them.'

Aubrey was walking beside her and added his own warning. 'You will not wander off and neither will you dance with any gentlemen that I haven't approved of.'

There was already a stream of carriages pulling up in turn outside the house – there were also several groups on foot, as they were. Aubrey nodded and smiled but didn't volunteer to introduce her to any of these people.

There was a red carpet spread down from the steps onto the pavement, which she thought rather ostentatious, but kept her comments to herself. Even though the walk was short the girls and herself had worn evening cloaks, which they handed over to a waiting maid. She looked around with surprise.

'There is no one here to greet us. Are we to make our own way in without direction?'

'The invitation did state that it was an unceremonious supper party, Mary.' Aubrey raised an aristocratic eyebrow and she responded with a smile.

'I think everyone is in that room over there, Aubrey. Should we just go in or shall we wait until a footman comes to claim us?' Giselle seemed equally baffled by the informality of the evening.

'We shall follow the other guests who came in front of us. I find this all rather odd, but interesting nevertheless.' This time when Aubrey offered his arm she took it. Having a gentleman of his standing at her side would make things so much easier.

'Have you any idea which of these people milling about are the host and hostess?' she asked Aubrey quietly.

'I met them once. Lord Bridport is unremarkable but his wife is tall and thin and has a penchant for bright colours.'

Mary scanned the ballroom and immediately spied Lady Bridport. She was the only one dressed in purple. 'Come along, girls, we shall get your brother to introduce us to our hostess. Hopefully we shall then in turn receive introductions to some of the other guests.'

They were welcomed warmly but her ladyship, despite her bright attire, was rather vague and showed no inclination to behave as she ought.

'I thought that informal meant no more than a dozen or two guests – obviously, I am quite wrong in my assumption. Already there must be almost a hundred here. There are musicians setting up on the dais at the end of this room so there must be dancing.' Keeping the girls at her side was going to prove impossible in the crush.

'Find yourselves some chairs and remain there whilst I investigate. I'm sure there will be a room set aside for conversation, and another for cards – we might be better somewhere quieter until I have time to circulate and find suitable partners for you girls.'

She did as he suggested and once they were settled she had time to take stock of the other guests. Giselle touched her arm. 'Mary, some gentlemen are coming this way. I believe that one of them is known to me – he was at university with Aubrey. Unfortunately, I cannot recall his name.'

The trio, all immaculately clad in regulation black, two in knee breeches and stockings, and one in the more recent fashion of trousers and evening slippers, halted in front of them.

'Lady Giselle, I was speaking to your brother only this morning. He gave me leave to speak to you if we should meet.'

Mary felt disadvantaged seated, so she stood up and stepped in front of the girls. 'We have not been introduced, sir, so you cannot be here until Lord Aubrey returns.'

The young man turned an unbecoming shade of puce, mumbled an apology and turned to go. His companions seemed less willing to depart without speaking, but she fixed them with her best basilisk stare and they too retreated.

When she resumed her seat, she turned to Giselle. 'I apologise if that gentleman was an acquaintance of yours, my dear, but your brother must introduce them. They should not have come over as they did.'

'I felt quite sorry for them, Mary. You are quite frightening when you glare in that way,' Beth said with a giggle. 'They are all very attractive gentlemen; I do hope Aubrey thinks them suitable to be introduced to us.' A few moments later he returned and didn't look particularly pleased when she told him what had just happened.

'Grantham is a decent enough fellow, but I can't vouch for his friends. I'm glad you sent them away, Mary. I have made enquiries and it seems the itinerary for the evening is as follows – nothing at all is planned. There might or might not be dancing; there might or might not be cards. The only thing that is certain is that there will be a substantial supper served at nine o'clock.' He snapped his fingers and a footman jumped forward holding a tray upon which there were four glasses. 'I have champagne for us and orgeat for the girls.'

The ballroom continued to fill and soon the floor was awash with ladies in elegant evening gowns and gentlemen in black. 'I don't wish to remain seated when everyone else is on their feet. Girls, I think it would be safe to circulate as long as your brother remains at our side.' She glanced at him. 'As you have already experienced several Seasons there must be a dozen or more people here you could introduce to the girls.'

'I have just seen a family I am acquainted with. They have a plethora of daughters and sons, so once you have met the parent I'm sure she will be delighted to introduce you to her progeny.'

He offered his arm and again she was happy to take it. The girls took their position in front of them and he herded them across the crowded space.

'Lady Johnson, good evening to you. Might I be permitted to introduce you to a family friend, Mrs Williams, and my sister and cousin?'

The woman he had addressed was small and plump, beautifully attired, and the epitome of elegance despite her unfashionable figure.

'Lord Aubrey, I have not seen you for this age. Is the duke in Town?'

'He is in the north on business but will join us before the end of May.' He made the introductions and then Lady Johnson beckoned over her family. The Johnson girls were pretty little things and the young gentlemen were respectful and suitably in awe of Aubrey to pose no threat to their charges.

Giselle and Beth were absorbed in the family group and Mary relaxed for the first time since they'd arrived. Her intention was to retreat to the periphery of the ballroom where she could keep an eye on her charges without being obliged to converse with strangers or dance herself.

* * *

Aubrey watched his sister and cousin drift away and was satisfied they could come to no harm if they stayed with the Johnson siblings. He turned to speak to Mary but she was no longer beside him. From his vantage point he could see over most of the heads, but she was nowhere in sight. She must have gone in search of the ladies' retiring room.

This was most remiss of her. She should have told him of her intentions as the girls must not be left unsupervised. The musicians were tuning up – the dancing was about to start. Immediately the people thronging the dance floor began to file to the edges of the room. He lost sight of Beth and Giselle as he was inexorably pushed backwards towards the wall. As soon as the ballroom was clear, couples began to form sets for the country dance.

He shouldered his way to the edge where he could lean against a pillar and see everything that took place on the dance floor. His vigilance was rewarded when a few minutes later Beth and Giselle were led out by the two Johnson boys. They would be occupied for twenty minutes – longer if they danced a second time.

Knowing they were safe gave him the opportunity to search

out their missing chaperone. He was quite certain she wouldn't desert her role and would return directly from wherever she went. The retiring rooms were usually on the upper floor if the reception rooms were on the ground floor. He watched the exit to the ballroom but did not see her returning. Could something untoward have occurred?

He shouldered his way through the crowd and was about to leave in search of her when he saw her tucked away behind a pillar at the far end of the chamber. From here she had an excellent view of the girls dancing with the Johnson boys.

It made sense for them to stand together – this way he would not be obliged to stand up with any hopeful debutantes and he could scowl at any would-be partners hoping to lead Mary onto the floor. The first dance was coming to a conclusion as he arrived at her side. She quite misconstrued his arrival.

'I had not intended to dance, Aubrey, but as you have made your way over here so purposefully to ask me, then I will stand up with you just this once.'

He could hardly refuse to dance without appearing rude. 'If I am obliged to dance at all, then I would prefer it to be with someone with whom I am acquainted.'

'Hardly a gallant response, my lord, but a man of your tender years cannot be expected to have the aplomb of an older gentleman.'

He fixed her with a glare of mock severity. 'I'll have you know, ma'am, that I'm renowned throughout the city for my good breeding and impeccable manners. That being the case, I sincerely hope you are competent on the dance floor as I have no wish to be shown up.'

She nodded regally. 'I can assure you, sir, that I have danced with dukes and princes in my time and none of them had cause to complain.'

The girls had decided to dance again with the same partners and he led her to the end of their set. The musicians struck up again and he was forced to admit she had not been exaggerating her prowess. He was quite disappointed when it ended and was tempted to ask her to dance again. In the melee, he lost sight of Beth and Giselle. 'Can you see the girls, Mary?'

'I cannot. They will have returned to Lady Johnson, I am sure.'

They were making their way towards the Johnson party when her fingers dug into his arm. 'Aubrey, did you give permission for them to dance with anyone else? They are being led out by the two gentlemen who accompanied your friend to this party.'

He swore under his breath. She was right – they were being escorted by Bishop and Dunstan. To his dismay Bishop was leading Giselle into a different set from the one that Dunstan had taken Beth.

'There's nothing we can do about it at the moment. However, we must separate the girls from those two gentlemen as soon as may be. They appeared pleasant enough, but for some reason I didn't take to either of them.'

'Then we are in agreement on this matter – I did not like them either. They are too worldly for our girls.'

* * *

Giselle seemed less impressed by her partner than Beth was with Dunstan. Sir Richard was smiling and whatever he was saying to her was making her smile. Their progress down the ballroom was attracting attention. They made an attractive couple: he with his dark hair and she with her corn-coloured curls.

Mary wasn't sure what it was about him that made her uneasy, but she definitely didn't want Beth with him any longer than this single dance. 'Aubrey, you must go across and insist on dancing with Beth once the music stops. She can hardly refuse. I don't think your sister will dance again with Bishop as she doesn't seem particularly enamoured with him.'

His arm tensed beneath her fingers. She shouldn't have given him an order but requested that he do as she bid. The matter was too important to worry about his sensibilities.

'That is an excellent suggestion, ma'am; how kind of you to give me such clear instruction.'

She removed her hand but managed to hold back her pithy response. 'In which case, my lord, I shall join Lady Johnson. I'm sure both girls will eventually rejoin that family group.'

He didn't deign to answer but prowled along the edge of the ballroom, waiting for the music to stop. She remained where she was in order to see if he was able to prise Beth away from her unsuitable partner. The poor girl was given no option – her cousin arrived and all but shouldered Sir Richard out of the way.

Beth looked more startled than upset by this abrupt change of partners. Aubrey took the girl to the head of a new set and by the time the next tune started they both seemed quite satisfied with the arrangement. Indeed, Beth was talking animatedly and appeared as happy in his company as she had been before.

As she was turning away, Mary's attention was caught by Sir Richard. He was almost hidden behind one of the marble pillars and possibly thought himself unobserved. His face was a mask of fury and a shiver of apprehension ran down her spine. She wasn't sure if his anger was directed towards Aubrey or towards Beth – but in either case she believed it possible the family had made a dangerous enemy.

The remainder of the evening passed without anything of note occurring. Aubrey returned Beth to the group and the girls only danced with the Johnson boys.

'Mrs Williams, your charges are quite delightful. They are ideal companions for my girls. Would you permit them to spend time with Lydia and Arabella? We have taken a fine house in Hanover Square for the Season, which is only a short distance from here.'

'I think that an excellent idea, my lady. Lord Aubrey will have to give his approval, of course, but I am sure he will have no objection. Perhaps Lydia and Arabella could come tomorrow morning for a visit? The girls have been asking to go to the Tower and see the wild animals in the menagerie. If we take two carriages, we could go together.'

They parted on good terms and Mary promised to send a note around to Hanover Square once she had spoken to Aubrey. The footmen were waiting outside with their torches to escort them back – although this wasn't strictly necessary as the lights from the waiting carriages were more than sufficient to see themselves over the short distance.

Beth and Giselle retired immediately but she wished to speak to Aubrey before she went out. 'There are matters we must discuss. Shall we go into the drawing room for a while?'

His smile was somewhat chilly but he strolled beside her into the chamber. 'We must not delay long; we are keeping the staff from their beds and they, unlike ourselves, have to rise at dawn.'

Did he think her ignorant of these facts? Instead of sitting down as she intended she stalked to the centre of the carpet and faced him. 'Lady Johnson would like our girls to go to the Tower with them tomorrow. Do we have your approval for this expedition?'

'Of course you do – there's no need to involve me in these trivial matters. If that is all—'

'No, it is not. What do you intend to do about Sir Richard and

Mr Dunstan?' She had not intended to speak so abruptly but it was too late to repine.

'I intend to find out more about both gentlemen. It was an unfortunate coincidence they had an invitation to the same party that we did.'

'No coincidence, sir, you must have mentioned it when you were drinking with them at your club.' She had no notion if this was correct; it just seemed the logical explanation.

His lips thinned and his eyes were arctic. 'Madam, you are mistaken. Are you so ignorant of the way things are in Town? Even if they had gained that knowledge from me – which they didn't – they could not have attended without having a prior invitation.'

She was now as cross as he was. 'You are wrong. Lady Johnson and I discussed this very thing. She pointed out several gentlemen who she knew had come without a formal invitation. All they had had to do was announce themselves at the door to be allowed inside.'

This was not going well and it was not entirely his fault. She was a mature woman, he little more than a stripling. She raised her hand as if in surrender. 'I beg your pardon, Aubrey, I have the headache and this makes me short-tempered. I am certain you will do whatever is required to keep the girls safe from predatory gentlemen and there is no need for me to mention the matter again.' She dipped in a formal curtsy. 'I bid you good night, my lord.'

7

The trip to the Tower was judged a success by all who participated. Over the next few days the four girls were inseparable and Mary began to feel herself redundant. Lady Johnson was an amiable lady but tended to treat her as if she was one of her charges.

Aubrey had been dining at his club so they hadn't had the opportunity to clash again. She had received another letter from her mother demanding to know what was happening in London. Mary decided to reply to this the next day as she would then have more to talk about. Tonight was the first major event in the social calendar and she would be able to describe the ensembles of members of the *ton*.

There had been no word from the duke but he was still expected to arrive in time for the ball to be held for Beth and Giselle – this would take place in two weeks. Preparations for this event were well in hand and everyone who had been invited had replied in the affirmative. This meant there would be more than two hundred guests to cater for.

There had been no morning callers, which surprised her as

she thought the etiquette was for any man who had danced with a young lady to call the following day to pay his respects. The only person who could answer this conundrum was Aubrey and she was pleased to see he had also come down early. He looked magnificent in his evening finery and she was glad she was dressed in one of her new ball gowns.

'Good evening, Aubrey, are you ready for the fray?' She dipped in a formal curtsy and he responded with a bow.

'I'm pleased you're here before the girls. There's something I need to talk to you about.' He gestured towards the little-used anteroom and she followed him inside.

'I too have something to ask you, but I shall speak of it afterwards. What's wrong? Is it the duke?'

'No, Beau is perfectly well. I have been making enquiries about Dunstan and Bishop and am most perturbed about what I discovered. Neither of the gentlemen has a feather to fly with – they are both hoping to marry money.'

'I thought that could be the case. I've spoken to the girls and warned them to avoid dancing with either of them again. Giselle was happy to comply but I fear Beth is already intrigued by Sir Richard. We must be vigilant tonight and make sure he doesn't get the opportunity to approach her.'

'I hope I have made it impossible for him to attend any of the prestigious events. They have no invitation to the ball we are attending this evening...'

'They had no invitation to the party last week but they still attended. If there are as many guests invited as there are at the one to be held here, then it will be easy for them to slip past the footmen at the door. Dunstan is tall and dark, as are many gentlemen, and will be indistinguishable as you all wear black.'

For once he seemed unbothered by her interruption and nodded. 'You are correct. I can think of no way to stop them getting in if they are so inclined apart from stationing myself by the front door.'

'If you do that then the girls will be free to interact with any other unsuitable gentlemen who might be present. There is nothing we can do about it, apart from stay close to them the entire evening. Unfortunately, when either of them are dancing it's impossible to know if anything untoward is taking place between them and their partner.'

'In which case, Mary, we will have to scandalise the tabbies and dance every dance together so we can keep an eye on them from the floor.'

She was about to protest at this outrageous suggestion when she saw the twinkle in his eyes. 'You are lucky, sir, that I do not hold you to that rash promise. I believe I can hear them coming. Do you think it would be sensible for you to remind them again that they cannot dance with anyone until you have given your permission?'

'I intend to do that. But looking as beautiful as they both do I rather think I might find it impossible. They will be the most sought-after partners tonight.' He started to turn away and then paused. 'Might I be permitted to say, that you also look lovely in your ensemble and are as likely to be as in demand as the girls.'

Her cheeks coloured at his compliment and she was relieved she could busy herself with fussing over the girls to hide her discomfiture from him.

In the carriage he issued his stern command. 'Do I make myself clear? If you disobey me then you will be taken home at once and not allowed to attend another ball for a week.'

This threat was sufficient to make both girls promise not to do anything rash. Beth smiled at Mary.

'I hope you are intending to dance too. It would be a shame not to parade your beautiful gown in front of everyone.'

'I shall dance if I'm asked by anyone suitable. I'm not so enamoured of the pastime that I would accept an invitation from any gentleman—'

Aubrey interrupted her this time. 'I'm afraid that's not how it works, my dear. The lady must dance with whoever asks her first – if they have been introduced of course – if she refuses anyone then she cannot dance at all.'

'That's quite ridiculous. I'm sure there will be plenty of ladies there who do not wish to dance every time. I can't believe that one must either dance the entire evening or sit out.'

'Lady Johnson discussed this with us the other day. What you cannot do is refuse to dance with one gentleman and then immediately take to the floor with someone else. Aubrey, you have quite misunderstood the matter,' Giselle said firmly.

'I stand corrected – or to be more accurate, I sit corrected. I did think it a strange rule. So, Mary, you may dance or sit out as you please. But remember, I have first claim on your hand so do not accept anyone else.'

* * *

Mary looked somewhat startled by his comment and Aubrey regretted speaking so enthusiastically about dancing with her. He much preferred the company of younger ladies, though not as young as Beth, and being with Mary somewhat unnerved him. She was so much more experienced than him – had been married for several years, whereas he had scant experience in the bedroom.

Apart from one quick fumble in a hayloft with a willing dairymaid several years ago, he was as innocent as his sister. Was it this that made him feel awkward when talking to Mary? Did she judge him as inadequate compared to her dead husband?

It had not been a conscious choice to remain celibate. It had just happened. He had no wish to father a clutch of illegitimate children and neither did he wish to set himself up with a mistress as several of his friends had done.

Indeed, Beau had a beautiful ladybird established somewhere in Town. She was the relict of a wealthy baronet and not a member of the *demi-monde*. The lady in question had chosen to be the lover of the Duke of Silchester with no expectations of becoming his wife. Aubrey had met her a couple of times at informal supper parties at the house and found her amusing and intelligent.

His reverie was rudely interrupted by Mary tapping him sharply on the wrist with her ivory fan. 'My lord, you are woolgathering. I swear you didn't hear a word I said to you just now.'

He smiled ruefully. 'I apologise. Would you care to repeat it and I will give it my full attention?'

'I merely said I should be delighted to dance with you.'

'In which case, Mrs Williams, shall we make our way to the ballroom? The girls have already gone ahead of us and I wish to ensure they are with Lady Johnson.'

He held out his arm and she placed her gloved hand on it. One could not fail to be aware of the interest their passage was creating. He wasn't vain enough to think it was him that was causing such a stir. He glanced down at his companion and she batted her eyelashes at him like a debutante and he couldn't restrain his chuckle.

'You are outrageous, madam, and are setting a poor example for our charges.'

'I wish to make you smile, sir – you are looking rather grim and we were attracting far too much attention. I'm sure people must have been wondering if you were displeased with me for some reason.'

'On the contrary, I'm delighted to be in your company.' He lowered his head so he could speak quietly into her ear. 'It is you they are looking at. Despite your venerable age, I believe you might be considered a diamond of the first water dressed as you are tonight.' The remark was not meant to be taken seriously. For a horrible moment he thought she had misconstrued his words as her fingers tightened on his arm.

'It is not me who is being outrageous. Please don't say anything else to force me to collapse into a fit of the giggles and disgrace both of us.'

There was no further opportunity for badinage as they had arrived in the ballroom. Immediately he saw Beth and Giselle. 'We can relax; the girls are fluttering about with their friends.'

She stiffened beside him and he looked down. 'What is it? What has upset you?'

'I'm certain I saw Dunstan lurking behind a pillar over there.'

All desire to laugh vanished. 'Join the girls, my dear. I shall wander over there as if looking for a friend. I can assure you that if he's here it is without an invitation. I shall suggest to him that he leaves quietly. However, if he doesn't then I shall get him ejected by force.'

Her smile made him feel ten feet tall. 'I hope I was mistaken, but I have excellent eyesight and doubt that I was.'

He watched her move gracefully to join Lady Johnson and her party before strolling, in what he hoped was a relaxed manner, in the direction she had indicated.

He reached the far side of the chamber without seeing his quarry. Then he saw Dunstan disappearing towards the card rooms. This would not do; this would not do at all. How the devil the villain had got past the vigilant doorman he'd no idea as he certainly didn't have a valid invitation.

He nodded and smiled his way through the crowd, keeping

his eyes fixed on the exit through which Dunstan had gone. The card room was busy. The hardened gamblers were already seated, piles of coins in front of them. There was no sign of the man he sought. Someone called his name. 'Lord Aubrey, you looking for someone?' It was an acquaintance of his.

'I'm looking for Sir Richard Dunstan. I was certain I saw him come in here. I have urgent business to discuss with him.'

Another of the gentlemen at the table gestured over his shoulder. 'He scuttled off in that direction, my lord. I don't think he wishes to be found.'

Aubrey nodded his thanks and strode off, determined to get the blackguard ejected. The door led into an empty passageway. He paused before deciding which direction to search. There was a slight sound behind him and then there was a searing pain in the back of his head and his world went black.

* * *

'Where has Aubrey gone?' Giselle asked Mary.

'He thought he saw a friend he wished to speak to. I'm sure he'll be back soon.' Mary turned to admire the Johnson girls and complimented them on their outfits. They were wearing identical white ball gowns as were most of the other debutantes present.

Giselle and Beth had selected pastel shades, and this made them stand out from the crowd. There were far too many young bucks hovering in the background, obviously hoping for an introduction to the loveliest girls in the room.

'Lady Johnson, I fear we are about to be overwhelmed by gentlemen wishing to be introduced to your daughters and my charges. Do you know any of those standing by that pillar?'

'I do indeed, Mrs Williams. Three of them could be considered eligible bachelors, but the other two are unknown to me.'

An Unconventional Bride 71

She turned to her sons who were talking earnestly to Giselle and Beth. 'Boys, are you acquainted with the redheaded gentleman and the one with ridiculously high shirt points?'

'Yes, Mama, but they are both impoverished and on the lookout for a wealthy bride,' the eldest of them replied.

'In which case, Charles, I'm relying on you to send them about their business as Lord Aubrey appears to have deserted us. You may tell the others to come forward so that they might be introduced to your sisters, and to Lady Giselle and Miss Freemantle.'

Introductions were completed in a flurry of bowing and curtsying and then the musicians began to tune up for the first dance. 'Lady Johnson, could I ask you to keep an eye on my girls? I'm becoming concerned about Lord Aubrey's continued absence and wish to assure myself that nothing unpleasant has taken place.'

Her companion looked surprised by this comment. 'I saw Sir Richard and his lordship went to investigate.'

Immediately Lady Johnson's expression showed her concern. 'Go at once, my dear. That man must be sent about his business.'

Mary hurried off in search of Aubrey. The card room was full. Both ladies and gentlemen were sitting at the tables, but there was no sign of the ones she was looking for. She drifted through the crowded chamber and departed by the door that was standing ajar at the far end.

The passageway was empty, the sound of the music faded as she closed the door behind her. Where did this lead? It was too well-appointed and spacious to be a route used solely by servants. He was obviously not here, and she could hardly perambulate around this house as if she were a member of the family.

She was about to return to the main reception rooms when something on the polished floorboards caught her eye. She moved closer to investigate. Her stomach lurched and her knees all but gave way beneath her. She was made of sterner stuff than this. She was the widow of a brave soldier and a little blood should not give her a fit of the vapours.

Something nasty had occurred here and she had a horrible sinking feeling that all was not well with Aubrey. He would have returned at once to take care of them all unless something had happened to keep him from their side.

There were two doors on either side of the passageway – one she had just come out of so had no need to investigate. It seemed sensible to look in the chamber nearest to the blood splatter. She pushed open the door and allowed her eyes a few moments to adjust to the darkness within. What she needed was a candle but she could hardly go back into the ballroom and demand one.

The wall sconces were too high for her to reach up and push one in, even if she had such a thing about her person. She had told Lady Johnson she wouldn't be more than a few moments and had no wish to alarm the girls by remaining absent any longer than necessary.

She stood in the doorway and listened, but could hear nothing. At the next door she opened, she did the same and was about to close it when she heard a slight groan.

'Aubrey, is that you? It's black as pitch in here and I cannot see to come to your aid.'

There was a muttered curse and then he spoke from the darkness. 'That bastard struck me on the head. Where the devil am I?'

'In a side room. Stay where you are; I'll send for assistance.'

'No, just give me a few more minutes and I'll be able to stand. I can see perfectly well from the light in the passageway.'

If he had been knocked unconscious he could well be suffering from a concussion. Returning to the ballroom was not an option – she must get him home as soon as possible and send for the family physician.

She stepped into the room and could see him slumped against the far wall. She dropped to her knees beside him. 'You must remain where you are. I'm going to remove your neckcloth and use it to bandage your head. You are losing blood from your wound and that needs to be stemmed as soon as possible.'

He seemed incapable of making a coherent answer but managed to raise his hand and touch her arm. She was skilled in ministering to injured soldiers and deftly wrapped the makeshift bandage around his head. She had been careful to keep herself and her gown clear of any blood splatter but realised her gloves would be beyond repair.

There was a candlestick on the mantelshelf and she snatched it up and then dragged a chair outside so she could stand on it and reach the sconce. Once she had done this she returned to his side. His face was ashen, but his pulse was steady. Hopefully he would make a full and speedy recovery once he was safely in his own bedchamber.

Whatever his views on the subject she must summon assistance and try and do so without attracting too much attention. There was a bell above the mantelshelf and she tugged it several times. The staff would be surprised to receive a summons from a little-used chamber but she hoped someone would come to investigate.

Whilst she waited she made him more comfortable with a cushion from a *chaise longue*. Fortunately, there was a rug folded neatly on a chair and she draped this over him. Using the one candlestick, she ignited several others and soon the room was fully illuminated. The clatter of footsteps outside heralded the arrival of the much-needed assistance.

Two footmen rushed in and slithered to a halt. 'Lord Aubrey has been struck down by an intruder. Arrange for our carriage to be brought around immediately. We will need a trestle upon which to transport him.'

They hurried away to do her bidding and whilst she waited she stripped off her gloves and pushed them into her reticule. Her next task was to get a message to Lady Johnson. She examined her appearance carefully and was sure there was no evidence of the accident on her gown. Apart from the missing gloves she was as elegant as she had been before she discovered Aubrey.

8

Mary stepped into the card room half expecting to be the centre of attention. However, apart from a few nods and smiles as she passed through the tables, she was more or less ignored. The ballroom was as gay as ever, the music as jolly, the couples swirling around the floor in a kaleidoscope of colour, and yet for her everything had changed.

She hurried across to join Lady Johnson who appeared unbothered by her prolonged absence. 'My lady, Lord Aubrey has met with an accident. He fell and hit his head and has a concussion. I must return to Grosvenor Square with him. Could I prevail upon you to take care of my girls?'

'Mrs Williams, what a dreadful thing to happen. Of course I will chaperone Miss Freemantle and Lady Giselle. My boys will ensure they are not pestered by undesirables. Shall you be sending the carriage back to collect them when the event is finished?'

'It will return immediately and be waiting to be summoned. I shall also send my dresser to act as chaperone on the return journey. I would not be sanguine for them to travel alone in a carriage so late at night.'

'What do you wish me to tell them when they get back from dancing?'

'Tell the truth – it is an accident and not a serious one. I'm sure Lord Aubrey will be up and about in a day or so, none the worse for his experience.'

Mary returned to Aubrey and this time she was sure her passage was noted. She really should have asked directions to the room that didn't involve her walking through here. As she reached the door she was aware there was someone behind her.

'Mrs Williams, forgive me for speaking to you when I've not been introduced, but I am a friend of the duke and could not help but be aware that something is amiss.' A tall gentleman with sandy brown hair bowed to her. 'Lord Rushton, at your service.'

'Come with me, my lord, and I shall explain it all to you.' Now was not the time to ask him how he was aware of her identity – that could come later.

Quickly she told him what had taken place and that she was certain Dunstan was behind the attack. 'I cannot fathom why he should wish to do this. All he had to do was slip away unnoticed and now he will have the wrath of the Silchester family on his heels.'

She led him inside the chamber and was dismayed to find Aubrey still comatose. This time she had a complete disregard for her gown and knelt beside him. His pulse was no weaker, but he was too cold, too still, for her liking.

'I don't like the look of him at all. I shall send for the physician to attend him here. I don't think he should be moved.' Rushton was beside her on the carpet.

'I have experience in these matters, my lord, and I give you my word it will do him no harm to be taken to his own apartment. He will do much better being looked after by his own people.'

'Then I will have to take your word for it, ma'am. Good – I can hear the trestle coming.'

* * *

Lord Rushton insisted on accompanying her in the carriage and she was mystified as to why he thought he should intrude in this way. She settled back with Aubrey's head in her lap and something prompted her to question his lordship's unwanted involvement.

In the darkness of the interior he was hidden from her view so she felt emboldened to speak her mind. 'I'm curious, sir, as to how you knew my name and why you thought it necessary to accompany us.'

'His grace asked me to introduce myself and offer my support in his absence.'

From nowhere she found herself defending Aubrey. 'I cannot see why the duke thought Lord Aubrey would be in need of assistance. He is more than capable of taking care of us all without the intervention of strangers.'

'I beg your pardon, ma'am, I was not implying that his brother was in any way derelict in his duties. Although, in the circumstances, you might be grateful for my involvement. I intend to search out this Dunstan and see that he leaves London immediately.'

'I thank you, sir, but I would prefer it if you left such matters to the family to deal with.'

A definite chill pervaded the atmosphere. 'As you wish, Mrs Williams. I have no desire to intrude.'

The remainder the journey was completed in silence and she

was relieved that he didn't offer to come inside. 'The carriage will convey you to your destination, my lord, before returning to collect Lady Giselle and Miss Freemantle.'

He bid her a stiff goodnight and she left him to return to the carriage. She cared little if she had offended him; her concern was for Aubrey.

She was walking beside the trestle and almost tripped over her feet when he spoke to her. 'I've no wish to remain in here, sweetheart, for apart from a thumping headache, I'm fully recovered.' To emphasise his point, he snapped his fingers and the four footmen carrying him quickly put down the trestle.

Aubrey was on his feet immediately. 'There, as you can see there's no need to summon the physician.'

Mary took his arm just in case he wasn't as well as he believed. 'In which case, you must allow me to deal with the injury. I'm glad you are able to walk unaided; I was envisaging you sliding from the trestle as it was carried up the staircase.'

* * *

Aubrey had come to in the carriage. For a moment he was disorientated but then recalled how he had come to be struck down by an unknown assailant. His head was resting in Mary's lap and there was someone else in the carriage – but he was certain it wasn't one of the girls.

When the other occupant spoke, he recognised this as the voice of one of Beau's friends, Lord Rushton. Mary's robust defence surprised and delighted him. He decided to pretend to be unconscious until they were alone.

When he revealed he was awake and quite able to stand up, she hadn't castigated him for his pretence but had taken his arm and gently teased him.

'Take me to the study; you can attend to my injury there. I've no wish to retire.' She guided him into the room and once he was seated she hurried out in a swirl of silk to fetch what she needed.

Whilst he waited he mulled over the events of the evening. Dunstan had obviously found his way to the ball, but whether his intentions had been to further his acquaintance with either Beth or Giselle he had no notion. What didn't make any sense was for the man to have attacked him.

He swung his feet onto the sofa, settled back and closed his eyes. Despite his protestations that he was perfectly well, that wasn't quite accurate.

He was roused from his stupor by the return of Mary, accompanied by his valet. She didn't engage in silly chit-chat but got on with the job like a professional. She had obviously sutured wounds before and it made him wonder about her life when she had been the wife of the colonel of a regiment.

After a while the tugging and discomfort ceased. 'There, sir, I am done. You have a concussion, but I don't believe it to be serious. Your head wound will heal in a few days, but you must rest in the interim.'

A goblet was pressed against his lips and obediently he drank the contents. It was watered wine and perfectly palatable.

'Your valet and a footman are going to assist you to your apartment, sir. They will settle you and keep me informed as to your well-being.'

The wine appeared to have restored him somewhat. 'Before I go, Mrs Williams, we need to talk.' Turning his head was painful but not impossible. He gestured to the waiting servants and they left the room. 'I can't remain in bed until I have discovered why Dunstan felt it necessary to attack me.'

'That has been bothering me too and perhaps I should have allowed Lord Rushton to investigate for us.'

'No, you were right to refuse his help. Although I'm certain he will ignore your instructions and poke his nose in anyway. He and Beau are very similar in that respect.'

'The only reason I can think of for Dunstan attacking you is that he didn't realise you had recognised him...'

'No, that won't wash. He was waiting for me – he must have seen me come into the card room. The worst that would have happened if I had accosted him was that he would be removed from the premises. Why would he risk his neck to avoid that happening?'

He leaned forward and picked up the silver cup, which she had thoughtfully refilled. He drained it. He wasn't sure if his head was spinning because of the alcohol or his injury. Whatever the reason, he needed to be in his bed.

'You must go up at once, Aubrey. There's nothing either of us can do about it at the moment.'

She must have called the servants back but he didn't hear her. Then he was half-carried, half-walked to his rooms and had never been more glad in his life to be divested of his garments and put in his nightshirt. His head was spinning unpleasantly and hurt like the very devil.

He closed his eyes and knew nothing more until the next morning when he was woken by the sound of his curtains being drawn back. Sunlight streamed into the room, making it unpleasantly bright.

'Leave them shut, Wells. Help me to the commode – my need is urgent.'

Once re-established in his bed he felt a little better. 'What time is it?'

'A little after eleven o'clock, my lord. Mrs Williams has enquired after your health and I was able to assure her that you slept soundly and your injury has not bled again.'

'I've no wish to malinger here. Don't look so horrified, man; I've no intention of getting dressed. Kindly pass me my robe and assist me to my sitting room. I wish to speak to Mrs Williams and cannot do so whilst in here.'

Aubrey had eaten a light breakfast and drunk another two goblets of watered wine by the time Mary knocked on his door. For some unaccountable reason he was desperate to see her although he had nothing new to discuss.

* * *

Mary remained in the drawing room until she heard the girls come back – the clock on the mantelshelf had just struck two when they returned.

'I take it you enjoyed yourselves, my dears. I beg your pardon for abandoning you, but Aubrey tripped and knocked himself out and I was required to act as his physician.'

'Is he badly hurt, Mary?' Giselle asked anxiously.

'No, a slight concussion and a few stitches. He will be back on his feet in no time. I shall accompany you upstairs, girls, and I don't expect you to rise until midday. No doubt there will be a stream of morning callers, so make sure that you put on your prettiest gowns.'

Beth threw her arms around Mary's neck. 'I've never had such fun, Mary. Thank you so much for bringing me. I danced every dance but have no idea of the identity, or names, of most of the gentlemen. I promise we were introduced and Lady Johnson gave her approval.'

'In which case, my love, I'm sure nothing untoward took place; you have grown up a lot since you got here and I believe I can now trust you to behave yourself. Come along, you must retire. We have kept the staff up long enough.'

***

The following morning she completed her ablutions and was dressed by eight o'clock. Having only a few hours' sleep was nothing to her – when they were on manoeuvres the regiment had sometimes marched all night. She wished to visit Aubrey and make sure he had not developed a fever. There was always a danger a wound could become infected, however careful one was when cleaning it.

She knocked loudly on the sitting room door and was invited to enter by Aubrey himself. She pushed the door open and was delighted to see him lounging on the daybed. His colour was good and his eyes were clear and bright. She had not noticed before they were an unusual shade of blue, so dark they were almost black.

'Good morning, I'm glad to see you looking so well. However, I believe that I told you to remain in your bed for two days.'

He grinned and gestured to a chair that had been already placed rather too close to his position. 'There's no need for you to check my wound; Wells has already changed the dressing and declared it healthy and healing well. I have only a headache to show for my adventures.'

'At least you have not got dressed...' She stopped, horrified she should mention something so indelicate as his being in his nightwear even if he was perfectly respectable.

He ignored her embarrassment. 'I intend to remain as I am until this evening, but I can assure you I shall be downstairs to dine with you all. Do you have plans to go out?'

'We have accepted an invitation to a musical evening tomorrow, but today we remain at home. The girls enjoyed themselves and I am expecting a plethora of morning callers later today.'

'Are you not going to sit and talk to me for a while? I'm sure if you leave the door open we will not be breaking any rules.'

She was being missish, not suitable behaviour for a woman of her mature years and experience. 'I should be delighted to remain here and converse for a while, but I warn you I shall leave as soon as I know breakfast is being served downstairs. I missed my supper last night.'

He waited until she was settled before speaking again. His expression was serious. 'I have enquiries in hand as to the whereabouts of Dunstan. I do not intend to have him apprehended for his attack as there is no real proof that he was the perpetrator. I'm still at a loss to understand what possessed him to do so. He can hardly approach either of the girls now.'

'I have been thinking about this as well. The only reason I can come up with for his extraordinary behaviour is that he was more concerned about being humiliated in public than he was about pursuing Beth or Giselle.'

He nodded. 'I think you might be right. That's the only sensible conclusion we can draw. He can have no grudge against me as I've only spoken to him the once. I have already sent word around to all the friends and acquaintances of this family to warn them to have him removed from their invitation list. After last night, I shall have him blackballed from the club.'

'If he wishes to marry wealth then he will have to move to the outer echelons of society – no doubt a wealthy cit with an eligible daughter might entertain his suit. After all, he has a title and an estate in Cornwall.'

'I pray that you're correct. It will make these next few weeks more pleasant if we don't have to worry about either him or his friend. By the by, have you had word from the duke?'

'He is still intending to be here to lead Giselle out at her ball next week. I shall have the privilege of taking Beth. Carstairs informed me the theme you have chosen is a traditional one – floral arrangements to complement the girls' ensembles.'

She had no wish to discuss something so mundane. 'To return to our previous discussion, do you consider it possible Dunstan has learned of your having him become a *persona non grata* at all the best houses?'

'Good God! That's it. It explains why he took the opportunity to strike me down.' He sat up straighter. 'He deliberately allowed me to see him knowing I would investigate. He found his way inside for the sole reason of injuring me.'

For a moment, she was speechless. 'Are you suggesting he tried to murder you?'

His eyes widened and he shook his head and obviously regretted it. When he had recovered from his dizziness he smiled. 'Not at all. He would not be so stupid. Injuring me was his aim, and in that he succeeded.'

'Then the threat from him is over? Now he has had his revenge he will leave us alone?'

'I am sure of it. In future, we can go to an event without worrying about him.'

She remained a while longer before leaving him to the morning paper, which had just been brought up on a silver tray. She had no expectation of seeing either Giselle or Beth before noon, but she had plenty with which to occupy herself.

At three o'clock she and the girls were waiting in the drawing room in the expectation of receiving a stream of morning callers. There were two maids presiding over the tea urn and Cook had excelled herself today. There were dainty almond biscuits aplenty – more than enough for two dozen visitors.

9

'I am quite exhausted, girls. I do believe we had more than thirty visitors this afternoon. Did any of the young gentlemen appeal to either of you?' Mary believed she had drunk more than five cups of tea and eaten far too many of the biscuits.

'Is it essential that we select ourselves a husband this Season?' Beth asked as she flopped down on the daybed.

'Of course not, my dear, you are here to enjoy yourself. If by chance you meet that certain someone, then you might well wish to think about marriage. I know a lot of young ladies contract a marriage for status or wealth, but I advise you to follow your heart. A union without love will be miserable for both partners.'

'Will you marry again one day, Mary?' Giselle enquired.

'I hope so, but finding a gentleman I could love as much as I loved the colonel will be an all but impossible task. To return to my original question – are you interested in any of the callers?'

The girls assured her they were not and she was satisfied they were in no danger of making an unsuitable alliance. They knew nothing of the conversation she had had about Dunstan with Aubrey and intended it should remain that way.

'We must return to our rooms and change for dinner. There is no need to put on an evening gown; something more informal will be correct for dining *en famille*.'

She was down before the girls and was unsurprised to find Aubrey there before her. He was dressed in his usual attire of buff unmentionables, boots and a dark blue jacket.

'Where is your bandage? I don't think you should have removed it so soon.'

'I've no wish to alarm the girls. I give you my word that Wells will replace it when I retire this evening.'

She took a glass of dry sherry from the tray waiting on the sideboard. She had developed a taste for this Spanish drink when on the Peninsula.

'I expect word reached you about the prodigious number of visitors we had this afternoon. We were quite overrun. There are at least three hopeful gentlemen – two interested in Giselle and one in Beth. Don't raise your eyebrows at me, sir; I can assure you none of them are any danger to our girls. They are not interested in forming an attachment at the moment.'

'I won't be able to accompany you to the musical evening tomorrow. However, I intend to come to the next major event on the social calendar regardless of the fact that I might still have stitches in my head.'

'Fortunately, there is only a second musicale this week. The next ball is not for a few days and they will be removed by then. Then it will be our ball – I can scarcely credit how quickly the time has flown.'

The evening passed pleasantly enough and they were all more than ready to return to their apartments without waiting for the tea tray to be brought in. Giselle and Beth retired first, leaving her alone with Aubrey.

'I missed my morning ride today. I do not intend to do so

tomorrow. Perhaps, when you are able, you would consider accompanying me? Although I always have a groom in attendance, I should feel happier with you alongside as well.'

The invitation had been extended because of her concern that Dunstan might still be a threat to the family, not because she had any desire for his company. He misunderstood her completely.

Something she recognised as interest flashed in his eyes. 'Thank you, I should be delighted to come with you. At what hour do you ride?'

'At first light – that way I can be certain of having the park to myself. Goodnight, Aubrey.'

* * *

He watched her go, enjoying the sway of her hips and her graceful carriage. Despite her mature years, she was still an attractive woman. Was she interested in a liaison with him? Surely not. He pushed down an image of her in his arms. Mary was almost a member of the family; Beau would skin him alive if he thought he harboured improper thoughts about his guest.

Aubrey was smiling as he returned to his bedchamber. Maybe it was time he looked for a ladybird of his own and set her up in a suitably discreet house. There was a club, more a den of iniquity really, where such introductions took place.

Tomorrow night, whilst the girls and their chaperone were otherwise engaged, he might consider going there to see if he could find a young woman to his taste. But the thought of being physically involved with a woman of the night didn't really appeal to him. Beau had a mistress, but she was a member of the *ton* who had chosen to form a liaison with his brother because she had no wish to remarry.

When the duke eventually arrived at Grosvenor Square, Aubrey vowed to find a moment to discuss this delicate matter with him. Having improper thoughts about Mary was not appropriate. He was surprised it was not the delectable Beth that filled his head. Since being with them she had become more sensible and even lovelier.

He was awake with the lark and even his vigilant manservant was not yet up. Aubrey was quite capable of dressing himself when needs be and was soon attired in his riding clothes. He emerged from his chambers as she was leaving hers. Her look of astonishment made him smile.

'Good morning, Mary. As you can see I am eager to join you for a gallop around the park. Which of our horses do you prefer?'

The skirt of her habit, a becoming shade of russet, was hooked over her arm and she was holding her gloves and whip in the other hand. 'I'm surprised you haven't noticed the arrival of a new mount in your stables. I had something purchased especially as I'm quite particular in my requirements.'

'I've not had occasion to go into the yard until this morning – I've used the carriage or my own two feet when I've been out. I'm eager to see this animal for myself, as I thought we had an excellent stable and that you would have been able to select something to your liking from what was already here.'

She hid her smile behind her hand and a flash of annoyance spoiled his good humour. What had he said to have caused her amusement? He was about to demand an answer when he understood. 'Tarnation take it! The blow to my head must have addled my brain. The only horses we have in Town are those we bring with us from Silchester Court.'

'Exactly so, which is why I decided to acquire my own mount.'

The maids had barely finished scrubbing the floor when they arrived downstairs. There were no footmen lurking about waiting to open doors and run messages and he was obliged to do the honours for them himself.

'I'm not sure you should be gallivanting about the place so soon after your injury. Do you still have the headache?'

'No, apart from the tug of the sutures if I move my head too quickly, I'm perfectly well.'

As they approached the stable yard they could hear the grooms taking care of the horses. She had walked briskly ahead of him, hadn't waited to take his arm, as eager as he to set out on their ride.

His horse, a tall chestnut gelding appropriately named Reynard, whickered a greeting. The animal was being held by a groom. The only other animal waiting was one he recognised as belonging to his family – presumably for the use of the groom.

There was the sound of a horse kicking the door of his stall and to his astonishment Mary ran towards the racket. 'Enough of that, you ridiculous fellow. Did you think you had been forgotten?'

She vanished into the stable and emerged leading a massive grey. The beast reminded him of the rocking horse he'd had when he was in the nursery – only a giant version.

He moved towards her and immediately the horse's ears went back and his teeth flashed. 'Cloud doesn't like men, my lord, so I suggest you keep your distance.'

She tied the horse to a metal ring and tacked him up herself. Two grooms handed her each item but were careful not to approach the flashing teeth. This was hardly a suitable mount for a lady.

'Have you taken leave of your senses, ma'am? What possessed you to purchase a horse that will not allow a groom to attend to it? Surely you haven't been taking care of it yourself?'

She glanced over her shoulder and then continued to tighten

the girth on the saddle. 'He's quite content to allow a stable boy to groom and muck out his stall. But Jonny has to stand on a bucket in order to tack him up, so it's easier if I do it.'

This didn't answer his first question about why she'd bought this animal in the first place. He thought he would leave this conversation until they were more private. What he intended to say to her on the subject was better said away from prying ears.

She led Cloud to the mounting block and nimbly climbed into the side-saddle. He followed suit, as did the groom, and once they were ready he touched his heel gently to Reynard and his horse moved off smoothly. He kept his distance from her horse, expecting it to lash out with his hooves if they came within distance.

'You can ride alongside me, sir. He enjoys the company of other horses. I think he was badly treated by his previous owner, which is why he reacts so violently to men.'

Aubrey did as she suggested and sure enough the two animals appeared happy in each other's company. The groom remained a discreet few yards behind them, which allowed him to resume his questioning.

'That horse is too big for you. Good grief, he is taller than Reynard and certainly broader.'

'Apart from his dislike of men, he's a gentle giant. Not only is he obedient to bit and heel but also responds instantly to my voice. He would have gone to the knacker's yard if we hadn't bid for him, as he had savaged three prospective buyers, as well as the unfortunate groom in whose charge he was.'

They had now reached the entrance to the park and whereas his mount was shying and skittering sideways in excitement at the prospect of a run across the grass, Cloud was perfectly composed and ignoring the antics of his equine companion.

So early in the day the park was deserted. 'Do you wish to race?' Mary asked.

'Not here – it's too close to the street and we might be observed. I recall there's an open stretch of grassland half a mile ahead. I'd be happy to see which of these horses is the fastest once we get there.'

She nodded and her horse moved into a collected canter and he had great difficulty keeping Reynard settled beside him. By the time they reached the open land he was fighting for control, whereas she was completely in command and looking decidedly smug about it. Something in the copse of trees to the left of the pathway caught his eye and for moment he was distracted. He was almost sure he'd seen a figure lurking there.

* * *

Mary settled herself more firmly and clicked her tongue. That was all that was required for Cloud to surge forward in a pounding gallop. Within a few strides she was several lengths ahead of her companion and the further they went the bigger the gap became.

She was revelling in the sensation of being the winner of the race when the chestnut nose of Aubrey's horse slowly inched past her boot. She urged Cloud faster and he responded gallantly but, despite his best efforts, Reynard drew level and they thundered past the last stand of trees with neither of them being the victor.

She sat back in the saddle and pulled gently on the reins. 'Enough, old fellow, slow down now.' The combination of her soothing voice and the tug on the bit was sufficient for her horse to shorten his stride and reduce his speed until they were walking. It took Aubrey far longer and he was obliged to circle Reynard before he regained complete control.

'My word, what a magnificent beast you have there, Mary. I thought he would outrun us.'

'I thought I would win. I didn't think there was a horse in London capable of beating us.'

'Apart from my mount, I doubt that there is. I have wagered hundreds of guineas on races and Reynard has never let me down. He might be a bit excitable, but he does love to race.'

Mary remembered they had set out with the groom. 'Where is the man who came with us? I cannot see him anywhere.'

'He's got more sense than to gallop after us. He will be waiting near the gates for our return.'

In order to cool the horses, they walked the mile or so back to the start of their mad race. The third time he looked at her in a most particular way, she began to feel uncomfortable. A well brought up young lady would not have felt obliged to comment – but she was a soldier's widow and did not follow convention.

'Is there a smut on my nose, sir? You have been looking at me so often I feel there must be something about my appearance that you dislike.'

His smile made her feel quite odd. 'I don't believe that you have noticed your hair has come down and your hat is long gone.'

She raised a hand to her head in surprise. 'Botheration! I particularly like that military-style hat. I cannot ride through the streets in such disarray.'

'I don't see why not; I think you look...' He stopped and cleared his throat before continuing. 'I think you look quite charming.'

The errant groom appeared in the distance and if she wasn't mistaken he was carrying the missing object. 'Look at that – my hat is arriving. If I can put my hair up again and restore it, nobody will be any the wiser.'

She knotted the reins and dropped them on Cloud's neck.

'Walk on, old fellow,' she commanded and he shook his head and his ears flicked back and forth. Now able to use both hands she managed to gather up her hair but as half the pins were missing she found it an impossible task to get it tidy.

Reynard was suddenly so close her boot was pinned against his flank. 'Allow me, sweetheart, you will never do it on your own.' Without a by-your-leave Aubrey removed his gloves and draped them across his knee and then gathered her hair and deftly plaited it. She was too surprised to complain and he too quick to be stopped.

'There, I have secured the end of the braid so it should remain tidy until you can get your maid to attend to it.'

The groom was now within earshot so she merely nodded her thanks and sent Cloud into a jog so she could collect the missing headgear. The groom handed it over without comment and politely turned his horse to face the exit whilst she pinned it back on.

'It is a tad unusual for a lady of my mature years to appear in public like this, but it is better than having it wild around my head as it was before.'

As the horses fell into step once more, he stretched out and touched her arm. 'You refer to yourself as if you were in your dotage – I swear you do not look a day older than my sister. Exactly how old are you?'

She tried to look cross at his impertinence and failed dismally. 'I shall be seven and twenty in May. Which makes me several years your senior I believe.'

'My apologies for asking such a question. I was four and twenty last month so the age difference is minimal.' He drew himself up and looked alarmingly like the duke. 'You are a beautiful young woman, Mary, and I will not allow you to refer to yourself in such derogatory terms again.'

She was strangely touched by his vehemence but thought it better to make matters quite clear before he imagined himself falling in love with her.

'I thank you for your compliments. Whatever the age difference, my dear, we are a world apart. I was married at seventeen and from the age of twenty, until my husband perished, I followed him across the Continent. I have seen things I would much rather forget. I was married for almost eight years and remained childless throughout that period. I have no intention of remarrying. I enjoy my independence and would not readily give that up again.'

He didn't look especially bothered by this solemn pronouncement. 'Thank you for the information. However, I cannot see why you thought it would be of any interest to me.'

She was shocked by his reply. Had she totally misunderstood his intentions? She turned her head and fixed him with her sternest look – one that had reduced insolent soldiers to quivering wrecks. 'My lord, if a gentleman refers to one as his sweetheart, then either he is a rogue or is showing an interest. I believed you to be the latter but obviously I was mistaken.'

Cloud broke into a rapid trot, not allowing him to reply. She remained at the side of the groom for the return journey, which meant he had to trail along behind. Hardly polite, but she had no time for such niceties.

10

Aubrey intended to explain to Mary she had quite misconstrued his intentions, but he could hardly do so in a public thoroughfare. This would have to wait until after they had both changed and broken their fast. He had been unaware he'd addressed her so familiarly and must watch his tongue in future if there was not to be a repetition of this misunderstanding.

There would be time whilst they were dismounting to request her presence in the study after breakfast. As they approached the archway that led behind the house to the stables she unaccountably increased her pace and had clattered inside before he realised what she was about.

A diminutive stable lad was already taking Cloud into his stall when he arrived and there was no sign of his quarry. Despite his annoyance, he was forced to smile at her ingenuity. She was as determined to avoid him as he was to speak to her.

He strode inside just in time to see her vanish up the stairs. He could hardly yell after her – although he was tempted to do so – and his opportunity was lost. He scribbled her a note and sent his man to deliver it before she could escape him again.

When he arrived at her sitting room door he was certain she had not already gone down. He knocked loudly and heard hurrying footsteps approaching. The door opened and her dresser curtsied politely.

'Mrs Williams is not receiving this morning, my lord.' The girl dipped again and closed the door, leaving him standing outside as if he was of no account.

He threw the door open and stepped in. Mary was standing by the window and she looked suitably shocked by his sudden entrance.

'I think you forget yourself, ma'am. This is my house and you are my guest. I will not be denied entry by a servant.' No sooner were the words spoken than he regretted them. His anger had made him behave badly. Immediately he started to reverse. 'I most humbly beg your pardon, I had no right to barge in...'

'And I had no right to refuse you entry. I know why you're here and I suppose we have no option but to discuss what took place earlier.' She perched herself on the edge of the window seat and gestured that he find somewhere to sit. He spun a hardback chair around, flicked aside his coat-tails, and did as she suggested.

They stared at each other without speaking for a moment. Instead of explaining he had no interest in her as he'd intended, he said something else entirely. 'Why is it that we cannot be alone together without falling out? I'm an equitable fellow not given to bad humour...'

Her delightful laugh filled the room and he couldn't prevent himself from joining in. The atmosphere changed from discord to harmony.

'Aubrey, I don't believe I've ever met a man so quick to fly into the boughs at the least provocation.' She shook her head and raised a finger like a schoolmarm as he was about to protest. 'Please, allow me to complete a sentence without losing your temper.' She quirked an eyebrow and he raised his hands in surrender. 'I was going to say, sir, I too have been behaving out of character. I must own that I've never met a gentleman like you before.'

He leaned forward. 'Is that a good thing or a bad?'

'I've yet to make up my mind. I am forced to own that you are lively company and I cannot remember having enjoyed myself so much for years.'

'I concur. Now, I suppose we must discuss the reason I'm here.' He looked directly at her and was surprised to see she was somewhat discomfited by his gaze. The careful phrases he'd rehearsed fled his mind and instead he spoke from his heart. 'We are like chalk and cheese, but we do agree on one thing. You have absolutely no interest in me as a prospective husband and I...' He'd been about to say that he felt the same but the words dried in his mouth.

'And you?' she prompted quietly.

His neckcloth had become unaccountably tight and he was finding it difficult to swallow. 'And I thought that I felt the same way but now I find myself drawn to you.' If he had stopped there all might have been well. 'I cannot understand it at all.'

Before he could react, she was on her feet and staring down at him. 'Can you not? I suppose it's because I am past my prime.'

He sighed and slowly got to his feet so they were standing no more than a foot apart. 'I've told you before, sweetheart, that you are a beautiful, young woman. An irritating, overexcitable one – but one cannot expect to have everything one wants in the same package.'

Her expression changed from cold to one of amusement. 'I have been called many things, but this is the first time I have been referred to as a parcel and...'

Now she was being ridiculous. He could think of only one

way to stop her continuing in this manner. He reached out and took her upper arms and drew her into his. With one hand firmly in the small of her back so she could not escape, he tilted her head with his other, and stopped her nonsense with his lips.

His intention had been merely to touch her mouth, but her scent, her softness against his hard contours made him forget himself and he deepened the kiss, expecting at any minute to have her stiffen in his arms and push him away.

* * *

Mary knew she should pull back and berate him for taking such liberties but something she recognised as desire flooded through her and she did the exact opposite. She pressed against him and softened her lips. His hardened and the tip of his tongue touched hers. Warning bells rang loudly. Things were getting out of hand.

She leaned back a little and instantly she was free. His eyes were dark; a hectic flush ran along his cheekbones. A rush of heat settled in her nether regions at the thought that she had roused passion in this young, attractive man.

His smile made him look older than his years. 'I should be on my knees begging your forgiveness...'

'Please don't – the gesture might well be mistaken for a marriage proposal and that would never do.'

He stretched out and gently stroked her cheek. 'Do you wish me to...' She held her breath. 'To apologise?'

'Certainly not. I am not an innocent young girl and I doubt my reputation will be besmirched by exchanging a kiss or two with an attractive gentleman.'

'In which case, my love, I believe matters are settled between us. In future I may refer to you as my sweetheart, or my love, and kiss you whenever we are alone.'

For a moment she thought him in earnest and then saw his eyes were alight with laughter. 'No doubt you will do as you please whatever I have to say on the matter. However, I think it would be wise if we avoided spending time alone together. I have no wish to become your mistress and you already know my opinion about marriage.'

He strolled towards the door as if nothing of any importance had taken place between them before answering. 'We Silchester men do not give up so easily.'

He was gone and she could hear him laughing to himself as he strode down the passageway. For a young man, he was very sure of himself. She had no option but to follow him as she was eager for her breakfast. On the way, she reviewed what had taken place and stopped so suddenly her toes were squashed against the end of her indoor slippers.

Whatever could he have meant by his last remark? Was he determined to persuade her into his bed or – even more unlikely – did he wish to marry her? The very idea was risible. He was the son of a duke, wealthy in his own right; why would he wish to make her his wife when he had the pick of this Season's debutantes?

Obviously, he wouldn't, therefore his intentions must be less than honourable. This was a conundrum she couldn't solve and she could hardly bring the subject up again. After all, she had already behaved with a disgraceful lack of decorum today.

She continued towards the hall, mulling over this puzzle. She was certain Aubrey would never behave in an ungentlemanly manner but she was equally sure she was the very last woman he would wish to marry. She was argumentative, far more worldly than him and, whatever he said on the matter, he was too young for her.

Her dearest Freddie had been almost twenty years her senior

and, if she was ever to consider a second marriage, it would be to a more experienced and mature gentleman. The fact that she found Aubrey so desirable was a worry – but she was not a flighty young miss and was perfectly capable of controlling her unsuitable inclinations.

In future, she would remain distant, revert to addressing him formally, and make sure she was never alone with him again. She sincerely hoped he would take his cue from her, otherwise things might become awkward between them.

When she got to the breakfast parlour he was happily munching from his laden plate whilst reading a newspaper. He ignored her when she came in and she wasn't sure if she was pleased or annoyed by this lack of manners. By rights he should have jumped to his feet and offered to collect her breakfast whilst she sat at the table waiting.

She piled her plate with a little of everything and took it to the far end of the table. He waited until she was seated before looking up. 'If you don't wish me to continue to yell then I suggest you remove to a more convenient position so we can converse like civilised people.'

He was behaving as if nothing out of the ordinary had taken place between them. She too could pretend they had not overstepped the bounds of propriety – indeed, that was the only thing she could do in the circumstances. If she continued to ignore him then both Beth and Giselle would become aware there was some restraint between their guardians, and she had no wish to involve them in this – whatever it was.

With her plate in her hand she made her way halfway down the table, but not into the chair adjacent to his. With a dozen sets of cutlery laid out, although there could only ever be four people eating, there had been no need for her to take her implements with her.

Once established in her new position she nodded cordially. 'I do not intend to ride out tomorrow in case you were expecting to accompany me.'

He seemed unsurprised by her announcement. 'That is fortuitous, as I have business to attend to in the country and will be away for one or two nights.'

She wasn't sure if this was merely an excuse to avoid her company or a genuine reason to be absent. 'The girls are to go to the musicale this evening. Are you content for them to attend or shall we send our apologies?'

'I see no reason why they should miss this event. Lady Markham is known to me and resides no more than a short distance from here. I have arranged for you to have two extra male servants accompanying you.'

He returned to his food, and she had no option but to do the same. She was sad she could no longer count on him as a friend and wished he hadn't stepped across the line and made things awkward between them.

* * *

Aubrey continued to eat as if he was unbothered by her presence when what he really wanted to do was put things right. She had made it abundantly clear she thought of him as a younger brother and not as suitable husband material. His business in the country was in fact to make a flying visit to his brother, Bennett, and ask his advice. If he wished to win the hand of the woman who had captured his heart, he would need all the help he could obtain.

He left immediately after breakfast not bothering to take Wells with him as he was only going to be gone overnight. He was riding as this would be quicker and Reynard was well up to making the journey twice in twenty-four hours.

He cut across the fields and was aware he would be arriving mud-spattered and dishevelled at the home of his brother and his wife, Grace. He reined in and Reynard dropped his pace to a sedate walk. He might be in disarray but there was no reason for his horse to be hot and sweaty.

His approach must have been seen as there was a groom waiting to take Reynard when he arrived in the turning circle. Grace must have seen him from the drawing room window and sent word to the stables. He bounded up the stairs and the door opened so he could enter without checking his stride.

The butler bowed. 'My lord, her ladyship is waiting in the green room to receive you. His lordship is absent but word has been sent to him.'

Aubrey handed over his hat, whip, gloves and coat and made his way straight through to greet his sister-in-law. She didn't rise on his entry but smiled warmly.

'Welcome, dearest Aubrey, and I apologise for not coming to greet you but I have been advised to rest. My pregnancy is not going as smoothly as one would hope.'

He dropped to his haunches beside her and embraced her fondly. 'I'm sorry to hear that, my dear sister. I beg your pardon for appearing in my muck – do you wish me to retire and repair my appearance?'

'Of course not – sit down and tell me why you have arrived in such a hurry.'

He didn't hesitate to explain his predicament; even though Grace was younger than him, she was years older in experience as she had been married for a year to his brother.

'I don't know how it happened, Grace. It must be something in the blood as so far all the Silchester siblings have fallen neck over crop in love within a week or two of meeting their prospective partners.'

'Mrs Williams will certainly make an unconventional bride, but she sounds ideal for you. She will keep you organised and you will keep her entertained. There is one thing I feel obliged to point out to you. She was married for several years and did not produce a child. This could mean you would never have babies of your own – are you prepared to sacrifice the joy of being a parent?'

'Her husband was an older man and I expect that was the problem. However, if we are not blessed with little ones so be it. I would rather live my life with Mary without children than with another woman and have a full nursery.'

'In which case, all we have to do is decide how best to persuade her to change her mind.' They were interrupted by the arrival of two footmen carrying trays with coffee, pies and pastries.

'Forgive me, Grace, I must remove the worst of my journey from my person before I join you for refreshments.'

When he returned, his brother was there. 'So, Aubrey, it would appear there is to be yet another wedding in the family.'

'I sincerely hope so, Bennett, but I've yet to convince the lady in question that I will make her a satisfactory husband. Do you have any suggestions as to how I can achieve my aim?'

He helped himself to food and took it to a chair by the window, allowing his brother and wife to sit together with a certain degree of privacy. They were so well suited, so obviously in love, and yet their romance had not started well either.

'There are other things I should tell you whilst we are together.' He regaled them with what had transpired and Bennett was immediately on his feet and striding across to examine the injury.

'It's healing well, little brother. I think the stitches can be removed in a day or so. I'm not comfortable with the girls and Mary being alone in Town. Have you still not been able to locate the bastard who attacked you?'

'I have men out looking for him, but as far as I can ascertain he immediately left London and is no doubt hiding out at his estate until the dust settles.'

'Why don't you return with Aubrey, my love. I shall be perfectly well for a day or two without you in attendance.'

'Absolutely not. I had a message from Beau yesterday saying he is finished with his business in Northumbria and will be beginning the long journey back today. He intends to spend a day or two at Silchester Court and will then come straight to Town. I'm sure Aubrey and the girls will be perfectly safe until then.'

Aubrey returned to the reason he had come in the first place. 'Thank you for your confidence, brother, but I'm at a loss to know how to convince Mary to change her mind.'

Bennett smiled. 'From what you've told me she is already interested but has yet to accept the inevitable. My advice to you is to continue as before – give her time and she will come to you without any further persuasion. Believe me, she wouldn't have allowed you to kiss her if she didn't have feelings for you.'

With that he had to be satisfied as the conversation moved on to more general things. Madeline was also in an interesting condition and the two babies were due in the autumn. If he wished to be married and have all his family present at the celebration, he had two options. One, postpone the event until next year, or two, expedite matters so they could be married in the summer. At the moment neither aspect seemed likely but he wasn't going to give up hope.

The following morning he left early, determined to reach Silchester House in time to change and join the girls and his beloved for the midday meal.

11

The musical evening comprised of a series of amateur performers, each more excruciatingly awful than the previous one. When Beth complained she had a headache and wished to go home, Mary was only too happy to oblige.

'Beth, you don't appear to be the only one suffering from some sort of malady,' Giselle said as their carriage joined a steady procession of similar vehicles pulling away from the venue.

'Why does anyone wish to play when they must be aware they are so awful?' Beth asked, having recovered remarkably swiftly from her ailment.

'I've no notion, my dear, but I am as relieved as you to be away from that caterwauling. I'm not surprised Aubrey had a sudden wish to visit the country; he must have known what to expect.'

'I'm glad to be getting home early. Tomorrow night is far more important – I heard they are to have fire-eaters and jugglers in the garden as well as fireworks when it gets dark.' Giselle settled more comfortably on the squabs before continuing. 'I do hope we have enough entertainment at our own ball. I don't want people to have recourse to invent an excuse to depart early.'

'I can assure you the ball will be a sad crush. You are the most eligible girls this Season and even if we offered nothing but indifferent refreshments, poor musicians and no cards people would still flock to Silchester House.'

The girls laughed at the thought that any of those dreadful things could possibly take place at their ball. From their chatter, it was apparent neither of them had formed an attachment to any of the young men they had met so far. Giselle was more than ready to embark on matrimony, if she met the right gentleman, but Beth was still too young in her opinion, and she hoped the girl would have a second Season.

Although she was determined she would not be her chaperone next time – she much preferred the tranquillity of her estate to the hustle and bustle of the city. This was odd as she had married dear Freddie in order to escape from the country.

The girls went to their repose and she retired soon afterwards. She had sent word to the stable that she would be riding as usual at dawn the next day and that her horse and a groom should be ready for her.

Her maid was waiting to help her disrobe. 'Jessie, please set out my habit as usual before you go. Ensure that my sprig muslin promenade gown with the matching parasol is ready for me to change into on my return.'

'Yes, ma'am, and I'll have hot water waiting too.'

* * *

The groom who was accompanying her on her early morning ride nodded gloomily at the heavy clouds. 'I reckon it's going to rain, Mrs Williams.'

'I expect it is, but not for another hour or two. I'll not stay out so long today as I've no wish to get drenched.'

Silver Cloud, always referred to as Cloud, seemed to sense the impending downpour. He was not overly fond of storms and Mary sincerely hoped there would not be one on this excursion. This was the only time he was difficult to control.

She kept her mount to a collected canter, not wishing to risk him bolting if there was a sudden clap of thunder or flash of lightning. The groom rode alongside her and this seemed to settle her horse. Then his bay gelding shied, crashing into Cloud, causing her to drop the reins and lose her balance.

The bay took hold of the bit and bolted. Cloud followed suit. There was little point in trying to grab the flapping reins. Desperately she wound her hands into his mane and tried to use her voice to calm him.

The groom had better success with his horse and as the bay slowed so Cloud did the same. Mary leaned forward and picked up the reins. 'Good fellow, good boy, easy now, easy.'

This time the horse listened and the huge animal dropped to a trot and then into a walk. The groom had lost his cap.

'Madam, I beg your pardon. Billy here saw something in the trees and caught me by surprise.'

'No harm done. We all survived the experience. Shall we go back and investigate what caused the upset?'

They turned the horses and walked them towards the copse where something had startled the bay.

'What exactly did you see?'

'I'm not sure exactly, madam, but I reckon it could have been a couple of footpads.'

'I don't see how it could be – they would have been unable to waylay us as we are on horseback, and I doubt that there would be any walkers so early in the morning.'

'It were here, but there ain't nothing there now. Do you want me to go and have a look?'

At that exact moment there was a distant rumble of thunder. 'No, we must return immediately if we don't wish to be caught in the rain.'

* * *

The weather worsened as Aubrey approached the city. He had no desire to be soaked to the skin so guided his horse onto the main thoroughfare and turned into the yard of a coaching inn not a moment too soon. A willing ostler took Reynard's reins and ran off with the gelding just as the heavens opened.

Aubrey made a dash for the door and collided with a gentleman equally eager to get out. The impact sent him staggering backwards and he only managed to keep his balance by grabbing hold of the door frame. The man he had crashed into was in no better case and ended up on his rear.

Immediately he stepped forward and offered his hand. To his dismay he saw that it was Bishop he had sent flying over. 'I beg your pardon, sir, I hope I have not injured you.'

The man scrambled to his feet unaided and looked decidedly shifty, not at all pleased to see him. 'Excuse me – don't wish to keep the cattle standing in this weather.' Bishop dashed past, and Aubrey watched him jump into a closed carriage pulled by two fine horses.

The landlord bustled forward wiping his hands on his apron. 'Can I be of assistance, sir? Are you desirous of a room?'

'No, I came to take shelter from the storm. I am sharp-set and could do with a hot meal and coffee if you have it brewing.'

The man bowed him into a wide alcove to one side of the main snug. Not quite a private parlour, but almost as good. A diminutive maidservant appeared at his side and stood waiting to receive his coat, hat, gloves and whip. When he draped the garment over her extended arms she was all but enveloped in its folds.

Somehow she managed a curtsy. 'I shall give these a right fine brushing, sir, and have them back to you in no time.'

Aubrey was glad of the fire burning adjacent to his alcove as, despite the fact that it was almost May, it was still cold when the sun was hidden by storm clouds. He had scarcely been seated five minutes when a potboy staggered in with a tray almost as big as himself. He thumped it down on the table with a sigh of relief.

'There you are, mister, steak and kidney pie made by the missus – you'll not find finer anywhere. There's a jug of coffee what you asked for and a nice bit of apple pie and cream for after.'

'I thank you. It certainly smells appetising.' He tossed the boy a coin and was left to his own devices. Also on the tray was a hunk of freshly baked bread, sweet butter and a dish of buttered carrots. He helped himself and was more than satisfied with his meal. He hoped Reynard was being treated as well in the stables as he was in the parlour.

The rain continued to hammer down and he resigned himself to an hour or two of delay at the very least. He drained the last cup of coffee and thought he would like another jug. He looked around for a bell, but as he could see no way of summoning assistance he got to his feet, intending to go in search of the landlord himself.

When he emerged from the light and warmth of the snug, the passageway seemed dark and chill. He had followed the landlord without taking too much notice of his surroundings and was at a loss to know in which direction to turn in order to retrace his steps to the vestibule.

He heard voices just ahead and decided that would be a sensible place to start. He stiffened as he reached the half-open door. Someone inside had just mentioned Dunstan's name. He paused outside, deliberately eavesdropping.

'I don't care, Pa, I ain't doing it, not even for Sir Richard Dunstan. And you don't want to get involved neither. If you don't take more care we'll have the Runners down on us.'

Aubrey couldn't hear the reply and could hardly linger any longer without being discovered. He reversed his steps and headed in the opposite direction. He found the maid and gave her his order. She handed him back his freshly pressed riding coat and other items.

He drank the coffee, lost in thought. What could Dunstan and Bishop be involved in that was illegal? If the two of them were actual villains, then it was hardly surprising Dunstan hadn't thought twice about knocking him senseless. Then his mouth curved at his nonsensical thoughts. A gentleman did not become involved with anything nefarious, even someone like Dunstan.

He tipped the staff generously before he left and his horse was waiting in the yard looking equally content with his short stay at this inn. The fields would be too wet and muddy after the downpour so he kept to the more well-travelled routes.

The house was quiet when he entered through the side door. The tall-case clock struck three and he thought that Mary and the girls might have gone out on morning calls. He confirmed this with the butler before heading to his own apartment to change his raiment.

'Wells, I'm going to my club. I shall require a bath before I do so.'

The best place to get information about anything from footpads to the latest crim con was at a gentleman's club. He wanted to be certain Dunstan was still hiding in Cornwall, even if Bishop was at large.

* * *

Mary and the girls returned from an extremely tedious afternoon of visits to a variety of houses in the most prestigious parts of Town. The girls were rather subdued on the return journey.

'Is something bothering you? Please tell me if there is and I'll do what I can to rectify matters.'

Giselle squeezed Beth's hand before speaking. 'Two people mentioned a rumour to us. I know we should not listen to gossip, but as it's about Beth you can understand why we are both so distressed.' She swallowed and dabbed her eyes with her gloved hand before continuing. 'Her name is being linked with Sir Richard. We were asked if an announcement was imminent.'

Whatever she had expected to hear, it certainly wasn't this. 'That's the silliest piece of tattle-mongering I've heard in a long while. You only danced with him once and we've not set eyes on him since.' She looked sharply at Beth who hung her head.

'Tell me you didn't meet him secretly.'

Beth looked up, her eyes brimming. 'No, of course I didn't. I'm not that much of a widgeon. He wrote me a most charming and flattering letter and I stupidly replied. I didn't say anything that could be misconstrued as an interest, but if he is showing the letter around as if it is a *billet-doux* then my good name is gone.'

'Tell me exactly what you did say.'

'I thanked him for his letter, told him I had enjoyed our dance together, and wished him well. I promise you, it was no more than that. It was a very short letter.'

'In which case, my love, you have nothing to worry about. Aubrey will be here tonight and he can make certain the truth is known. Dunstan is a rogue – he is trying to embarrass the family because Aubrey has made sure he will not be received in the best drawing rooms in Town.'

Her brisk reassurance was sufficient to rouse the spirits of the girls. When they arrived outside Silchester House they were as lively as usual. The butler informed her that Aubrey had returned and then gone out to his club, but would be back to escort them to the ball.

'Is my brother not going to be here to dine with us?' Giselle said.

'It would seem not, my dear. I'm sure it would be easier for us to dine upstairs and not put the staff to the bother of laying up in the dining room. The carriage will be outside at nine o'clock. I pray there will be no return of the unpleasant weather of this morning.'

* * *

She was writing a letter to her mother when she heard the unmistakable footsteps of Aubrey returning to his own chambers. She was across the room and called down the passageway before she had time to reconsider her impetuosity.

'My lord, I must speak to you most urgently.'

He lurched to one side and for a horrible moment she thought he was in his cups – then she realised her sudden appearance had caused his momentary unbalance.

'Devil take it, Mary, why must you shout like a fishwife down the corridor?' His bad language made her smile – and he was right to take her to task. She forgot far too often that she was no longer living under canvas surrounded by rough soldiers.

'Never mind that – are you coming or not?'

The rattle of a supper tray approaching made him look around. In this house the servants were encouraged to use the main staircase when carrying trays as the back passageways were narrow and precarious.

He sniffed appreciatively. 'If I may share your meal then I will join you. I haven't eaten for hours.'

'As we will be eating supper at the ball, I'm sure there will be more than sufficient for both of us. It will have to be brief, as I must start my preparations for the evening.'

The door to her bedchamber was ajar and Jessie was busy clattering about in there making her presence obvious. The sitting room door was also open and she hoped this was enough to stop unpleasant speculation.

She told him about the gossip. 'I'm relying on you to speak to everyone tonight.'

'I certainly will. I also learned something interesting today.'

He finished his story about the encounter with Bishop. 'I thought that I had overheard something to do with highway robbery but there has been none on that stretch of road. I don't understand how my friend Grantham became involved with those two villains – but he's a gullible sort of fellow and a bit slow in the attic.'

'Even if there had been incidents of highway robbery, the chance of either of them being involved is remote. I don't suppose we will ever know the significance of what you overheard. It is none of our business.'

He swallowed the last mouthful of his food and stood up. 'Are you still not riding in the morning?' His smile was wicked as he spoke.

'I rode this morning and almost came to grief.' She quickly explained what had transpired and he looked less than impressed.

'Then you have no choice, Mary; in future you either remain at home or accept my escort.'

She shrugged. 'In which case, Aubrey, I shall see you in the stable yard at six o'clock tomorrow morning. I'm sure an athletic young gentleman like yourself will manage perfectly well on three hours' sleep.'

He smiled at her riposte but didn't deign to answer. Although it was two years since she had followed the drum, she was still able to function perfectly well on very little rest.

When she was dressed, she hurried to the girls' chamber to admire their ball gowns. 'You both look lovely. I think white is so insipid and am glad we decided you should wear pastels.'

'You look beautiful, Mary. One might mistake you for an eager debutante tonight. That particular shade of blue, like duck egg shell, is perfect with your colouring,' Giselle said.

Their escort for the evening was looking equally splendid in his black. She was unsurprised to see he had adopted the new fashion of pantaloons and slippers rather than knee breeches and silk stockings. If she looked less than her years, then he looked older than his.

12

It took almost an hour to mount the red-carpeted stairs, curtsy to the family, and find their way into the main reception rooms. The girls were bubbling with excitement and immediately asked permission to join Lady Johnson and her family.

Mary looked at Aubrey for confirmation and he nodded. 'Run along, girls, we shall join you presently. I wish to admire the... the interesting decorations for this event before taking my place in the ballroom.'

Beth said. 'I do hope you intend to dance together again. You make a handsome couple.'

The two of them ran away giggling and Mary fiddled with her fan, hoping to disguise her pink cheeks.

'Don't look so anguished, sweetheart; no one could possibly link our names together. After all, I am the son of a duke and you a soldier's relic.' His teasing comment was exactly what she needed to recover her equilibrium.

'You, sir, are ridiculous. I have no wish to marry you or anybody else, but if I was on the marriage mart then I could do worse than set my cap at you.' She fluttered her eyelashes in what she hoped was a beguiling way.

'And you, my love, are quite outrageous. As you insisted you want to look at the outlandish objects that purport to be decorations, shall we do so?'

They were not the only couple strolling around the periphery of the ballroom exclaiming at the purple and yellow festoons that were draped everywhere. Prominently displayed amongst these hideous drapes were enormous golden bows.

'I sincerely hope these colours have not been chosen to match the gowns of the ladies of the house. Whatever can have possessed them? It will be the talking point of the Season.' Mary was doing her best not to smile.

'Perhaps that is the reason for these abominations. All the members of the *ton* wish to be talked about.' Aubrey stopped and nodded towards an enormous arrangement of purple and yellow flowers and dyed feathers. 'Remind me again, what is the theme for our ball next weekend?'

'There is no theme as such; we are having arrangements of summer blooms and there will be banners upon which have been written Giselle and Beth's names. These have been made from the same material as their gowns – primrose yellow for your sister and damask rose for your cousin.'

'That sounds admirable. Are we also to have a red carpet outside and dozens of flambeaux?'

'I fear so as it's expected of us. I suggest that we dispense with a formal greeting line. I cannot understand why this custom has continued when it obliges guests to stand about for hours just to curtsy to the family holding the event.'

'On that I must overrule you, my dear. You cannot deny our guests the honour of being greeted by the most prestigious Duke of Silchester. I expect that's the reason many of them are coming.'

She thought he was in jest, then she saw his face. 'Do you intend to stand in the line alongside your brother?'

'Good heavens, of course not. Neither will you – we can hide away in the study until the dancing starts.'

Every few yards he stopped to introduce her to someone or other but no sooner had they passed than she forgot their names. Eventually they reached Lady Johnson who had established herself behind two pillars halfway down the room. Somehow, she had managed to gather a dozen of the spindly gilt chairs for the use of her progeny and themselves.

'Good evening, my lady, this is going to be an interesting evening. Your girls look quite delightful.'

'I bid you good evening, Mrs Williams. I have heard a whisper that someone from the royal family is to attend tonight – that is why it's so crowded.'

Sitting in a ball gown was ill-advised as doing so would crease it abominably, so the girls were on their feet, which meant the young men were also standing. This made the cluster of chairs redundant. What it did provide, however, was a small oasis of space for them to occupy.

A stream of hopeful young gentlemen arrived to be introduced to the girls and the Johnson boys wandered off to be introduced to others in their turn. When the musicians struck up the first tune for a country dance two determined gentlemen headed her way.

Before either of them could ask her to dance, Aubrey took her hand and led her forward to join the first set.

'I don't believe I agreed to dance with you, my lord.'

'Yet here you are. I have no intention of introducing you to either of those fellows who were approaching. One is a hardened gambler, the other a rake.'

'Are you suggesting the only reason they wished to partner me was for my wealth? That is hardly gallant of you.' Her rebuke was not serious and he responded in kind.

'As you keep telling me, my love, you are at your last prayers.' Then his expression changed and she saw something she didn't recognise flash in his eyes. His voice deepened and struck a chord deep within her. 'So it could not possibly be they were attracted by your beauty, elegance and wit. Or the fact that, without a shadow of doubt, you are the most beautiful woman here tonight.'

She almost tripped over her own feet. She was unused to compliments of any sort; dearest Freddie had been a man of few words and with not a romantical bone in his body.

There was no time for her to ponder on these words as they were swept away in the dance and she was forced to concentrate on her steps as this was not a country dance she had performed before.

* * *

When the dance came to its conclusion, Aubrey was tempted to keep her out for a second set but common sense prevailed. 'Our charges are remaining on the floor. I fear if you return you will be pounced upon and have to dance a second time.'

'Heaven forfend such an event! Shall we repair to the card room for a while? It should be safe enough in there.'

'Last time I entered a card room it was far from safe.' He touched the back of his head, which was still sore although the sutures were now gone. 'Do you think there might be any disgruntled gentlemen waiting to strike me down tonight?'

She laughed and several heads turned in their direction. 'Oh dear – I believe we are being pursued by those two gentlemen from before who appear determined to snatch me away.'

The music began again and the danger was over. No one could take her away from him once the dance had begun. He couldn't spend the entire evening whisking her from room to room in order to avoid potential partners.

'I believe if you sit down with Lady Johnson you are less likely to be asked.'

'I should have worn a turban, then I would have been indistinguishable from the other matrons guarding their chicks from predatory gentlemen.' Her smile was enchanting. 'I believe I will dance tonight but only if I have been formally introduced.'

'I have no intention of introducing you to anyone. I shall speak to her ladyship on the subject and ensure that she does the same. I shall have no objection if you take to the floor with either of the Johnson boys.'

'You might not have, sir, but I believe the gentlemen in question might object. They consider me as an aunt and would find dancing with me an unpleasant experience.'

He could not remember having enjoyed so lively a conversation before. The more time he spent with Mary the better he liked her.

They returned to the ballroom just as the dance was reaching its conclusion. Giselle and Beth came back flushed and happy from their exertions.

'I intend to dance every dance this evening, Aubrey,' Giselle said as she gratefully took a glass of lemonade from a passing footman.

'I shall do so as well,' Beth added. 'However, I believe the rumours are still spreading as I've been receiving several speculative looks from the tabbies sitting around the room.'

Aubrey cursed inwardly. 'I apologise, sweetheart, I had quite forgotten. I shall circulate immediately and put an end to it.'

He was reluctant to leave Mary unattended, as without his

presence at her side he feared she would be beleaguered by eager suitors. She waved him away with a smile and he had no option but to depart.

He wandered around the establishment stopping and speaking to everyone he knew and mentioning Dunstan and his perfidy whenever the opportunity presented itself. He was sanguine Beth's name would no longer be linked with that villain after his intervention.

More than an hour had gone by before he was able to rejoin his party. Lady Johnson was chatting companionably to another chaperone but there was no sign of Mary or the girls. He scanned the two dozen or so couples skipping around the ballroom and immediately recognised both Beth and his sister.

'Lady Johnson, forgive me for interrupting, but do you have any idea of the whereabouts of Mrs Williams? I cannot see her.'

'Have no fear, my lord – Lord Rushton came across to speak to her and they have gone out to walk on the terrace.'

Aubrey nodded politely and shouldered his way through the press of people. Rushton was a handsome man, wealthy and a bachelor still. Did he have designs on Mary?

The terrace was pleasantly cool after the stuffiness inside. There were several couples promenading and it wasn't hard to distinguish the one he sought. There were dozens of flambeaux illuminating the area and in the flickering golden light he was relieved to see her standing a good two yards from Rushton.

He steadied his breathing and strolled across to greet them. 'Good evening, my lord, I hope I find you well.'

'You do, sir, you do indeed. I can see that you are fully recovered from your scrape last week. Mrs Williams has been telling me that Dunstan and his crony might well be involved in something nefarious.'

'I'm sure they are, but it's no concern of ours.' He closed the distance between himself and Mary, leaving Rushton standing on his own. He got the hint.

'I enjoyed our conversation, Mrs Williams. Excuse me, but I have agreed to play a hand of cards and am tardy.' He bowed and marched away.

'I'm sorry if I interrupted you…'

'I'm always pleased to see you, Aubrey, and you interrupted nothing of importance. Did you complete your mission?'

He told her how things stood and she was satisfied the matter was at an end. 'It's so lovely out here one would scarcely know one was in a city.' She sniffed and pulled a face. 'Apart from the all-pervading smell of smoke, that is. I long to be in the country where the air is fresh and I can ride for miles without meeting another soul.'

'I always enjoy my time in Town but, like you, I'm delighted to return home.' They were leaning against the stone balustrade and the sound of music drifted out from the open ballroom windows.

'Lord Rushton asked if I would like to dance or if I would prefer to walk on the terrace with him. I'm not sure if that was because he wished to spend time alone with me or because he thought me past the age of dancing.'

He chuckled. 'Fishing for compliments, my love? That is poorly done of you.' He held out his arm and without hesitation she placed her gloved hand on it. 'The next dance is the supper dance – will you accompany me to the ballroom?'

'I should be delighted to, but only if you desist from calling me your love. It's not that I object, but if you were to be overheard you might find yourself in an untenable position.'

* * *

She had expected him to look horrified, to insist she walk further from him, but he patted her hand. 'It is not I who has a reputation to lose if our names are linked.'

'Why should I be vilified? I rather think I shall be applauded for setting my cap at such a prize as you and then successfully ensnaring him.' She waited expectantly for his riposte.

'Ah ha! Is that the game you play, madam?' He smiled in a decidedly improper way and heat unexpectedly flashed around her body. 'Do you think to capture me with your wiles?' He bent his head and whispered in her ear. The warmth of his breath did nothing for her already unsettled composure. 'I shall expect your bedchamber door to be open to me tonight, my love.'

She couldn't hold back her shocked exclamation. To her chagrin, he laughed. He had been teasing and she had taken him at his word. She rapped him hard on his knuckles with her fan and was pleased when he winced. 'You must not say such things even in jest, sir.'

He was still smiling when they reached the ballroom. The country dance was in progress so she released his arm and made her way to Lady Johnson.

'My dear, when are we to expect an announcement? It is plain that you and Lord Aubrey are quite taken with each other.'

'Indeed, you are right, my lady, that I am fond of Lord Aubrey – but as a younger brother, not as a potential suitor. It is the same for him, I do assure you.' The lady looked unconvinced so Mary continued. 'I could not possibly consider a gentleman so much younger than myself and with so little worldly experience. I was happily married for many years to Colonel Williams and if I ever decided to marry again it would be to a gentleman like him.'

'I understand perfectly, Mrs Williams. You could do worse than look in the direction of Lord Rushton – I'm sure you could bring him up to snuff if you chose to.'

This was a highly inappropriate conversation and Mary was relieved when the dancing finished. Aubrey was at her side before the last bars had faded.

'This is my dance I believe, Mrs Williams.'

She put her hand on his arm and followed him. The sets were forming, but it would be several minutes before order had been restored from chaos and the dancing could begin again.

'So, not content with adding me to your list of conquests you are now to pursue Rushton.'

'You were eavesdropping, and it serves you right for hearing such nonsense.' She tilted her head so she could see him properly. 'Would you rather I had confirmed her suspicions? Can you imagine what your toplofty brother would have to say on the matter if he arrived to the news that you had just got yourself betrothed to me?'

'I know exactly what he would say. He would congratulate me on my good sense and wish me well. Why would he do otherwise?' This time his expression was serious, no hint of humour in his eyes.

'In which case, do you intend to make me an offer?' He raised an eyebrow and glanced around the crowded room. 'I'm quite happy to drop to one knee and declare myself, sweetheart, if that's what you would like me to do. However, I should much rather wait until we are alone.'

It was impossible to tell if he was in earnest or enjoying himself at her expense. He would never make an exhibition of himself in front of the cream of society. Knowing this prompted her to push the matter a little further.

'Yes, if you are really serious in your intentions towards me, my lord, you must prove it by declaring yourself immediately.'

'I will do so if you give me your word that you will accept me. I'm not making a cake of myself for nothing.'

This had gone too far and she had nobody to blame but herself for being in this embarrassing predicament.

'Please, Aubrey, don't be a nincompoop. You will humiliate your sister and cousin and make us the laughing stock of the evening.'

The musicians struck up the first note and whatever he had been going to say was lost as she stepped away to join the line of ladies who had to face the gentlemen for the duration of the dance.

Somehow, she completed the set without disgracing herself but was heartily thankful when she curtsied for the last time. She was hoping to escape – she had no wish for supper – but he was too quick for her.

'Lady Johnson promised she would claim a table large enough to accommodate all our party. We must make haste or others will take our places. Look – the girls are ahead of us.'

His arm was resting lightly around her waist as he guided her expertly through the crush and into the dining room. Beth waved her fan vigorously above her head in order to attract their attention. Unfortunately, she also decided to call out loudly.

'Lord Aubrey, Mary, we are over here. We have saved seats for you.'

Several matrons frowned and heads were shaken at such unbecoming behaviour. This would not do; this would not do at all. If Beth was to be censored for her exuberance then she too would share the same fate.

She waved gaily above her head. 'We are coming, thank you kindly for thinking of us.'

If Beth's behaviour had caused a murmur of disapproval, hers produced a stunned silence. This was broken by her companion, who didn't just call out, but yelled at parade-ground volume.

'I am sharp-set, Cousin Beth, and could eat a veritable horse.'

13

Mary was making a strange choking sound and Aubrey was concerned for a moment. Then he realised she was trying to hide her laughter behind her fan. He winked at her and this made her laugh harder.

Even Beth, who had started this farrago, looked a little startled by his behaviour. He guided his companion to the table and hastily they both sat down. By the time they had done so the buzz of conversation had returned to its normal level.

'My word, sir, that was quite unexpected. Forgive me if you think I am impertinent to mention this, but it's not the usual thing to shout at an occasion like this.' The plume in Lady Johnson's turban was waving wildly, such was her agitation at his outlandish behaviour.

'I do beg your pardon, my lady, I don't know what came over me. I can assure you I do not normally behave like an escapee from Bedlam. It must be the company I'm keeping that has temporally deranged my senses.'

He received another painful rap on his knuckles from Mary's fan. 'You are outrageous, my lord, to blame any of us for your extraordinary outburst.' She was still having difficulty controlling her giggles.

He nodded solemnly. 'Beth began this competition to scandalise the *ton*. Then you bested her and I could not allow you to be the winner. I wonder what prize I will receive for my efforts?'

'We shall be fortunate indeed if we are not asked to leave. We are receiving very peculiar looks from the other guests.'

Beth and Giselle were now giggling into their napkins and soon Lady Johnson was smiling too. A bevy of footmen began to circulate with silver platters laden with delicious items. They placed a selection on each table and then they were left to help themselves.

He could do with a stiff drink after all the excitement, but there were only jugs of lemonade on the table. Then more servants came around with claret and bottles of champagne. Soon the noise in the dining room made sensible conversation impossible and everyone was shouting to make themselves heard.

Instead of talking they concentrated on devouring every morsel of the supper. He was careful not to drink more than two glasses of claret and he noticed Mary took only one.

Her ladyship stood up and they followed suit. She led the way like a ship in full sail, her burgundy gown flowing around her ample frame. The ballroom was quieter now but still unpleasantly hot.

'I suggest that we take a turn around the garden for half an hour. The dancing won't start again until everyone has finished supper.'

The four young ladies and two young men dashed off in a flurry of petticoats and coat-tails leaving Mary, Lady Johnson and himself to follow along at a more decorous pace. A year or two ago he would have been with them, but now he was content to leave the giddiness to those younger than himself.

He couldn't prevent a chuckle escaping as he thought about his silliness in the dining room.

'I hope that sound doesn't indicate you are about to do something else you will regret in the morning,' Mary said softly. She was walking beside him as if she belonged there, although he would have preferred her to have linked her hand through his arm.

'I don't know why I did it... No, that's not true. You didn't want Beth to be embarrassed by her *faux pas*; I just joined in for the fun of it.'

'Whatever your reasons, I've never laughed so much in my life. All I can say is, that it's a good thing your brother isn't here because I fear he wouldn't have found the incident at all amusing.'

'Beau might be the Duke of Silchester, but he's not so high in the instep he can't enjoy the ridiculous. I rather think he would have exacerbated matters, not condemned our behaviour.'

'I suppose the girls will wish to stay until the final dance. As we have completed the two dances we are allowed by society's rules, I shall sit with Lady Johnson and refuse anyone who asks me to partner them. I suppose you will join your cronies in the card room.'

They arrived at the terrace. Her ladyship spied two friends and went to sit with them, leaving him to escort Mary into the garden. The blackbirds were singing their final songs, but he couldn't hear the intricate warbles of any nightingales. He would have to return to Silchester to hear those.

'The decorations inside are quite hideous, but they have made the outside space look like something from a fairy tale. The lanterns swinging in the trees and the ribbons tied around the trunks are quite delightful.'

She picked up the skirt of her gown and ran gracefully down

the central steps from the terrace into the garden itself. He had no option but to follow her. They weren't alone out here – even in the fading light, he could see other couples and groups of people enjoying the fresh air before they returned to the fray.

There was no sign of the Johnson siblings, Beth, or Giselle. 'I don't think it was wise to bring them all out here. I noticed that the young men imbibed several glasses of claret. I hope they don't misbehave now they are unsupervised.'

'I have spoken to your sister and Beth, and they assured me they thought of the Johnson boys as family members, not as possible suitors. I'm sure they will behave impeccably even though they cannot be seen if they did do something improper.'

They wandered through the rose garden and came across a secluded arbour surrounded by honeysuckle. She reached up to smell a blossom and her skirts became entangled in the rose thorns.

'Stand still, sweetheart; if you struggle you will make it worse and tear the material.'

* * *

Immediately she stopped wriggling and remained still. If she ruined her gown she would have to return; although she had protested about being obliged to remain, for some strange reason she didn't want the evening to end.

Aubrey was crouching at her ankles as he deftly released the silk. Several times his hands brushed her stockinged legs. By the time he had succeeded in his endeavours she was tingling all over. Her hand had crept of its own volition to rest on his snowy shirt front. His heart was pounding beneath her fingers and she was sure it wasn't from his exertions.

What happened next was inevitable – she swayed towards

him. His arms encircled her waist and drew her so close her soft curves were pressed against his hard contours. His kiss was nothing like anything she had experienced before.

When he eventually raised his head she was bereft and wanted to feel his mouth on hers again. 'My darling, I shall not apologise for kissing you.'

Before she could prevent it, he dropped to one knee and took her hands in his. 'Please make me the happiest of men, my love, and marry me.'

His words were like icy water being thrown over her head. Her pleasure in the encounter vanished to be replaced by dismay. 'Dearest Aubrey, there's no need for you to make the ultimate sacrifice. I'm not a green girl but an experienced woman. Please, get up at once, before anyone else observes you and draws the wrong conclusion.'

He rose smoothly, his face now that of a stranger, and not a particularly friendly one at that. He stared down his aristocratic nose at her. 'I see I quite misunderstood the matter, ma'am. I was under the impression that you were a lady and should be treated as one. I was erroneous in my assumptions. Forgive me – although you have offered yourself to me so charmingly I have no wish to make you my mistress.' He nodded curtly and strode off into the darkness.

She had made a sad mull of things and wished she had phrased her refusal in such a way that he wasn't so mortally offended. She remained where she was for a while until she was sure she had recovered her composure. As she stood listening to the evening birdsong the full import of his final remark struck home.

Her mood changed from dismay to fury. How dare he talk to her as if she was a member of the *demi-monde*? She would find him and tell him exactly what she thought of his behaviour. As she turned to leave, her skirt caught for a second time and this time there was the unmistakable sound of material tearing.

She moved into the circle of light from one of the hanging lanterns to examine the damage and knew at once she would have to return home. In fact, the tear was so bad she couldn't even go into the ballroom to explain to their party why she was disappearing.

Perhaps she could find a helpful footman and get him to take a message. She would also have to send for the carriage, which would no doubt throw the coachman and his assistant into panic. As she stepped back onto the terrace, Aubrey appeared from the shadows.

'This way, I've found a little-used door. You can't wish to go through the main reception rooms with your beautiful gown so torn.'

His manner was friendly, no sign of his previous opprobrium apparent. She didn't like to be at daggers drawn with him. She took his arm and he guided her through a passageway and into an empty anteroom.

'Thank you, I can wait here without fear of being embarrassed. Please send for the carriage, and could you take a message to the girls? Lady Johnson must once again act as chaperone in my stead.'

He nodded and strode off, leaving her alone to her thoughts – these were not happy ones. She had no option but to remain in London until the end of the Season, but what she would really like to do was take herself off to the country away from Aubrey.

She wandered around the room, picking up objects and replacing them without being aware of what she was doing. A considerable time later there was a polite tap on the door and a footman told her the carriage was waiting outside.

Her eyes filled. It was no one's fault but her own Aubrey was staying away from her, but he had come to mean far more than he should. She wanted to put matters right between them.

The journey back was short and she retired immediately. Jessie tutted and fussed over the gown.

'I doubt that I can mend this, madam, but I will do what I can.'

Once in the seclusion of her bedchamber, certain that her maid would not return that night, Mary let the tears fall. She had cried when darling Freddie had died, and she believed tonight that she felt quite as wretched as she had then.

Tears were for young ladies, not for a mature woman of almost seven and twenty. She sniffed, blew her nose and scrambled out of bed, now wide awake and regretting the fact that she was in her night garments and couldn't go downstairs to await the return of the girls. She was also hungry – it seemed an age since she had eaten supper at the ball.

There was sufficient light from the moon filtering in through the shutters for her to find the tinderbox and relight some candles. She was wide awake. The time was just after midnight – several hours before they came home.

There was a book she had obtained from their visit to Hatchards the other day that remained unread. She would curl up on the daybed in her sitting room and read until she heard them in the passageway. After reading for half an hour, Mary decided she would retire as she intended to get up the next morning to ride at dawn.

* * *

Aubrey deliberately kept away from Mary as he was aware he was becoming increasingly protective and possibly possessive as well. He had no wish to manipulate her into accepting him as a possible husband; she was as attracted to him as he was to her. However, desire was not enough on which to base a lifelong partnership.

His hope was that over time she would change her mind about him, and he was prepared to wait. They had only been acquainted a few weeks and had spent most of that arguing. He watched her from a distance as she slipped away to the carriage, holding the torn skirt of her gown together so her petticoats would not be seen.

Standing behind Lady Johnson in order to give his approval of any would-be dance partners was an essential but boring business. Once the girls were safely in a set he was able to wander off and make himself agreeable to any of his acquaintances he might bump into.

After a long and tedious couple of hours, the last dance was over and the guests began to depart. He had taken the precaution of ordering his vehicle a while ago so they would not have to wait an hour or more until it took its place at the end of the red carpet.

Even the girls were quiet on the short ride to Silchester House. They bid him a polite goodnight and, arm in arm, they made their way upstairs. He yawned and decided to do as they had and find his bed. He paused outside Mary's room to see if there was a flicker of candlelight coming from under the door. There was none, and her sitting room was silent.

Quite what he would have done if she'd been awake, he had no notion. The longcase clock at the end of the passageway struck three times. If he was to rise with the lark in order to accompany Mary on her ride he had better get to bed immediately.

His valet had retired several hours ago – he never kept him up so late. Aubrey was asleep the minute his head hit the pillow and didn't stir until Wells woke him as he opened the shutters and drew back the curtains.

'God's teeth! What time is it?'

'Seven o'clock, my lord.'

Aubrey leapt out of bed and dashed into the dressing room. He completed his morning ablutions in moments, ignored the shaving water, and pulled on his clothes as if the house was on fire. He took the servants' stairs as they were more direct, and erupted into the passageway, causing an unfortunate footman to drop the tray of cutlery he was carrying.

The resulting clatter brought the butler running, but Aubrey had no time to waste on this. He ran down the narrow corridor and out of the side door. On arriving in the stable yard he yelled for his horse to be brought out immediately.

'How long ago did Mrs Williams and her groom leave?'

'About an hour ago, my lord,' one of the stable boys replied.

Minutes later he was astride Reynard and trotting towards the park. She usually spent two hours on her excursion so with luck he would be able to accompany her for some of the ride. He urged his mount into an extended canter, expecting to see the two horses ahead of him.

He travelled the entire distance of her usual route without any sign of them. If she had come to the park, then they would have met by now. For some reason, this morning, she had gone in a different direction. She must have taken the right-hand path that led to the lake. This was more circuitous and even a collected canter would be risky.

Notwithstanding this danger, Aubrey travelled at high speed but failed to see either the groom or Mary. He reached the lakeside and scanned the empty shoreline. This was most perplexing. Somehow, he had managed to miss her, but he couldn't imagine why this had happened. There was no other route she could have taken.

The only explanation was that she had exited via the gate at the far end of the gallop, had decided to return through a different neighbourhood. This was a strange thing to do, but nothing to worry about. She would be at home when he got there and would no doubt apologise handsomely. No, that was quite incorrect. Why should she do this when she hadn't known he was looking for her?

He was smiling as he turned into the stable yard, eagerly anticipating a fiery exchange of words and an even more pleasurable reconciliation.

The head groom greeted him with a worried frown. 'Is Mrs Williams not with you, my lord? We expected them back a while ago. They are never away longer than two hours.'

Reynard was blown. He'd pushed him hard, and he couldn't expect this horse to go out again immediately. 'Saddle another mount for me. Get two men ready to accompany me. We must go in search of her immediately.'

14

Mary was about to leave for her ride when an urchin sidled up to her and slipped a note into her hand and vanished before she could ask from whom it came. She stepped to one side so she could read it in privacy.

Mrs Williams,

I have in my possession a packet of incriminating letters that were written by Miss Freemantle to Mr David Wiggins. If you don't want these to be put into circulation and your charge to be ruined, then you will follow the instructions in this note exactly.

Leave the yard as usual and draw no attention to yourself. There will be a closed carriage waiting on your route and you and your groom will enter it. Your horses will be taken care of in your absence.

The missives will be exchanged for something of value that you own. The choice is yours.

There was no signature. The reason she had removed Beth

from Somerset was because of her growing closeness to Wiggins, the son of the local squire, and even at three and twenty a hardened gambler. He must be behind this and would no doubt demand money when she arrived.

She didn't hesitate. Tommy, her usual groom, took her bent leg and tossed her into the saddle. There was no need to alert him until she spied the carriage. The two horses walked across the sleeping square and turned without prompting into the road that led to the park.

The carriage was just ahead. 'Tommy, we have to dismount and climb into that vehicle. Please don't ask questions. I need you to come quietly and do whatever is asked without protest.'

He frowned, but nodded. 'Right you are, Mrs Williams. I'll not do nothing to upset no one.'

The door was open and the steps down. She got into the gloomy interior half expecting the letter writer to be inside, but the carriage was empty. The blinds were drawn and when the door slammed shut it was hard to see.

Once they were in motion she told Tommy that she was going to recover some embarrassing letters, but didn't say from whom, or to whom they had been written.

'Right you are, madam. I'll keep mum about this. If we are back within two hours no one will know we didn't go to the park.'

'I hope that will be the case, but I think it unlikely. I believe you are with me so that you can take back a message. Money will be needed to reclaim this correspondence and that will have to be fetched from my bankers. Hopefully you will be able to return and set minds at rest. I have no wish for a search party to be sent out.'

The carriage turned onto a busy road and trundled along for some time before veering sharply onto a rutted track. The blinds

An Unconventional Bride 137

were fastened so it was impossible to look out and she had no notion where they might be now.

'I believe we are at our destination. You must remain silent whatever transpires. Do you understand?'

'Yes, madam.'

The door was pulled open as soon as they were stationary. A surly individual let down the steps and then gestured that she proceed along the weed-strewn path towards a dilapidated building. When her groom made to follow, he was prevented by the coachman and his henchman. They grabbed his arms and led him off in the opposite direction.

She walked, head held high, towards the house. The front door opened as she arrived but she couldn't see who was behind it.

The entrance hall was dark and smelt of damp and disuse. She was about to turn and speak to whoever was behind her but received a sharp push in the small of her back and was forced to keep moving. There was an open door ahead and she walked in. Her heart was hammering, her legs trembling, but no one would know this to look at her.

She marched to the centre of the room and spun around. Her bravado faded when she saw who was facing her.

'Welcome, Mrs Williams. I see from your expression that you were not expecting to see me.'

'Sir Richard, what is the meaning of this outrage? Have you taken leave of your senses?'

'In case you were wondering, my dear, I do have those letters. I bought them from Wiggins. Would you care to be seated?' He pointed at a ramshackle sofa and reluctantly she did as he suggested. There was no point upsetting him by being difficult.

She took the seat and he sat on a matching scruffy armchair opposite. 'Excellent. I said in my note that I was going to exchange these letters for something valuable. I wonder if you have guessed what that might be.'

'Of course. You want a substantial sum of money. That can be arranged. I shall need to send my groom to my bankers...' He was smirking at her and her stomach clenched. Had she misunderstood?

'Oh no, my dear, I already have my recompense. It is your reputation for Miss Freemantle's. A fair exchange, do not you think?' Casually he tossed over the letters, which landed on the floor at her feet.

Finally, the enormity of her situation registered. She was to be destroyed instead of Beth. Her mouth was dry. She could scarcely breathe. Did he intend to ravage her? She closed her eyes and tried to regain her composure.

'Whatever you do to me, I'll not marry you.'

His laugh chilled her to the marrow. 'Good God, I don't wish to tie myself to such a termagant. My intention is to see you are no longer able to marry anyone else. A Silchester would not look at soiled goods. I shall have ruined both your lives and be content.' His eyes gleamed and his smile did not reassure her. 'I might not wish to marry you, my dear, but I might wish to bed you. I've not decided yet.'

He stood up and pointed to the far end of the room. 'There is all that you need for your stay behind that screen. Make yourself comfortable. You will not be going anywhere for a day or two.'

'My groom? What of him?'

'If he does as he's told he'll come to no harm. He has your horses to take care of so he won't be idle.'

With that she had to be satisfied. He strolled out as if this was the most ordinary event in the world, leaving her life in tatters. The man was insane. Did he not understand the enormity of his actions? When Aubrey found him he would not survive the encounter.

She collapsed on the sofa and let the tears trickle down her cheeks. Her reputation was gone, or would be if she didn't return home soon. There was no doubt in her mind that she would be found but it would be too late. Aubrey would not marry her. No gentleman would.

She finally understood her feelings. She loved him and wished to be his wife, to become part of his large and loving family. This was impossible because, even if he was prepared to overlook her shame, she would not allow it. Marrying her would ostracise him from the world he lived in. She could not do that to the man she loved.

She used her sleeve to dry her face and stood up determined not to give that monster the satisfaction of seeing her broken. Whatever happened she would face it with fortitude. Her estates were substantial; she could live there happily unbothered by society. After all, had she not refused to marry because she preferred her independence? Until a few weeks ago the Silchester family had been unknown to her, so surely she could return to her previous existence without too many regrets?

Her first task was to destroy the letters. It was the work of minutes to see them merrily burning in the grate. At least that was one disaster averted.

Next, she must find something she could utilise as a weapon, for one thing she was sure of was that she would not allow Dunstan to assault her. Spending years as a soldier's wife had taught her a thing or two about fighting and this would stand her in good stead if she was attacked.

Behind the tatty lacquered screen was a commode, thankfully clean, and a bed already made up with linen and comforter. There was a nightstand upon which was a jug filled with cold water and a china basin. There was no soap and no towel; she would have to use her petticoats. How she was to manage her hair she had no notion, but somehow she would find a way to keep it tamed.

Her riding habit was made of a heavy cotton twill and it was uncomfortably hot in the stuffy chamber. The voluminous skirts, made to spread over the saddle, were not suitable for indoor wearing. If she could open a window or two her incarceration would be less unpleasant.

She tried but they refused to budge; either they were nailed closed or were too warped and old to move. The panes were dirty on both sides and ivy grew across the window, making it impossible to see out, and also dark inside.

She explored her quarters, hoping to discover a weapon or a book to read. There was no fire and therefore no poker or tongs. The three candles, unlit, were not in heavy candlesticks but in the shallow tin saucers used at night to keep the grease from the floors. Had he anticipated her intentions and made sure the room was without anything heavy?

Then, hiding behind the empty bookshelf, she discovered a small piece of wood. This was too small to inflict damage as it was, but if she could somehow sharpen it, it might serve as a knife. She doubted she was to be starved so there should be a knife arrive with her meal. They would be checking to see it went back with the crockery, but she could use it to whittle away at the wood in the interim.

There was nothing to read and the time dragged past. She started every time she heard a creak or scuffle, but these were only the sounds of rodents in the walls and the old house moving. The room was so gloomy she couldn't tell what the hour was by the amount of light coming in the windows. Her stomach gurgled several times so it must be well past noon.

Would someone answer her summons if she discovered a bell strap to pull? There was none. She banged on the locked door to no avail so abandoned the attempt to attract attention. She was obliged to use the commode and did so with trepidation, expecting the door to open whilst she was in an embarrassing position.

After further fruitless pacing she subsided on the sofa and attempted to sleep. Then there were heavy footsteps approaching and finally the door opened and the male servant came in with a tray.

'It ain't to your fancy tastes, but it's all you'll get today, so make it last.' He dumped the food on the sideboard. 'No point in banging on the door; no one will come. It's only me here until the master returns tonight.' He stomped out and she heard the key turn in the lock outside and then it was noisily removed. This was good news as it would give her ample time to fashion her wooden knife.

Mary examined what had been brought to her. It didn't smell too bad and actually looked quite appetising.

There was a tureen of thick vegetable soup, fresh bread, a platter of cold cuts, three slices of plum cake and a jug of lemonade. Even more importantly there was a sharp knife ideal for her purposes.

If she was to have no further sustenance she had better not eat everything, although she was hungry. The soup would be better hot, but the bread would keep, as would the cake. However, the meat might turn in the heat so she'd better eat that as well as the soup.

Replete, she carried the remaining food to the rear of the chamber and placed a dampened cloth torn from her petticoats over it. Then she sat with her back to the door so anyone entering would be unable to see what she was doing.

After an hour, the wood was carved to a sharp point and the shavings were carefully hidden under the bed. Pleased with her efforts, she pushed the makeshift weapon into the pocket of her skirt and returned to the sofa.

Dunstan was returning at nightfall and she could think of only one reason he would do so. No one could possibly wish to spend any longer than necessary in this dismal place. He must have designs on her person. She would be ready for him if he did come. Being a widow meant that she knew what was involved and this gave her the confidence to believe she could protect her virtue if she had to.

She prowled around her quarters, jumping at every creak and groan of the old house – but still no one came. The room grew dark as night fell and the two candles were barely sufficient to light the large chamber. Eventually she grew tired of waiting for a visitor who might not come and decided to retire.

As she was in the process of removing her skirt she froze. Was this what the villain wanted? She would be at her most vulnerable if in bed and only wearing her undergarments. With this in mind she reclined on the lumpy mattress fully clothed – even her riding boots still in place. The night was warm so she had no need of the comforter.

She slept in snatches, unable to rest easily, in case she had a nocturnal visitor. The welcome sound of the dawn chorus filled the room and with some relief she scrambled off the bed, made use of the facilities, and finished the remains of the food that had been brought to her the previous day.

Aubrey and the girls would be frantic with worry as she had now been missing an entire day and night. He might never find her here and she had no notion how long Dunstan intended to keep her incarcerated. If his objective had been to ruin her good name and make it impossible for Aubrey and herself to be married, he had already achieved his aim. She prayed that he would be satisfied with this, believe that he had already got his revenge on both of them.

There was no mirror in the chamber so she was obliged to arrange her hair as best she could by touch alone. When she pressed her ear against the door she could hear nothing – the house was silent. The servant had left her with the sharp knife. He would not have done so if Dunstan had intended to return. She had spent a disturbed night for no reason.

With this knife, and her makeshift weapon, she would attempt to prise up a window and make her escape. The wood splintered and even the knife made no impression on the nails that held it shut. Perhaps the glass would break in one of the small panes if she hammered at it. Firstly, she collected the blanket from the bed and then attacked the window with as much force as she could muster.

Something moved beneath her hands – it wasn't the glass but the leading that held them in place. She removed the blanket, draped it over her head and face, then threw herself bodily at the window. It gave way beneath her and she tumbled headfirst into the bushes below.

On scrambling to her feet, she checked to see if she had suffered any injuries from her unexpected exit. The debris from the glass and leading were safely embedded in the blanket. She was unscathed from her dramatic plunge. She remained silent, leaning against the house wall, listening for the sound of someone coming to investigate the noise. Nothing; she was safe to continue her escape.

She crept around the house towards the rear of the building where she assumed the stables would be. She intended to release her groom and hopefully the two horses as well. The search proved successful and after a few minutes she was poised, holding her breath, beside the stable block.

Yet again there was no evidence of human occupation, but she could hear horses moving around inside. Did she dare to call out in the hope of locating her man? No – she would tack up and lead them out so they were ready to be mounted at a moment's notice.

Cloud was ready and she was about to do the same for the other when the groom called out. 'Is that you, Mrs Williams? I'm locked in the fodder store – can you let me out?'

'Thank the good Lord, Tommy, I was praying I would find you and that you would be unhurt.'

In a matter of minutes the animals were ready and they led them out into the silent yard. 'I reckon it won't be full light for another hour, madam. We will be well away by the time anyone notices you have escaped.'

'I hope you are correct. I have no idea where we might be, but I don't think we can be very far from Grosvenor Square as we were not in the carriage for that long.'

He tossed her into the saddle and mounted himself. Together they made their way down the unkempt drive and out into the street. She looked around, hoping to recognise some landmark that would give her a sense of where she was.

Tommy stood up in his stirrups in order to get a better view. His expression turned from worried to relieved. 'Look over there, ma'am. Can you see the church tower? I reckon it could be the one we pass every morning on the way to the park. If we ride in that direction, we should get home all right.'

15

Beau was heartily sick of the never-ending problems pertaining to his northern estates. The tenant of his biggest concern had succumbed to the sweating fever, leaving the place in disarray. Then no sooner had this been rectified and matters put in order than he learned of two further disasters, one in Scotland at his hunting lodge, and another on a smaller estate near York.

Finally, he had resolved everything and could set out for London. The letters from his brother were sketchy and infrequent, but Rushton had also written, which helped fill in the gaps. It was a three-day journey to Silchester Court and he was eager to speak to his factor before joining Aubrey in Town.

It would appear that his friend was rather taken with Mrs Williams – that would be an advantageous match for her. At least the business with Dunstan had been resolved and the girls were safe from his predatory approaches.

Giselle, at nineteen years of age, was old enough to become betrothed but he was glad she hadn't settled on anyone as yet. His cousin Beth would make a welcome addition to the household with her lively behaviour. He had no adverse reports about

Giselle's injury so must presume being in London had made her forget about her damaged leg.

His home would be silent and lonely when the two girls eventually left to get married. Of course, Aubrey would return, but being a gentleman, he was free to come and go as he pleased. He had his own estate in Essex and might well decide to remove himself there.

Maybe his brother would fall in love with Beth – he had certainly shown an interest in the girl. Marrying a first cousin wasn't something he would recommend, but he wouldn't stand in their way if that was what they wanted.

He arrived at Silchester late on the third day of travelling. He had sent word ahead that he was coming so the house was awake and ready to receive him. He didn't linger downstairs but went to his repose immediately.

He had scarcely closed his eyes when there was a thunderous knocking on his bedchamber door. His valet was elsewhere so he must answer the summons himself. He slept naked, but always kept a bedrobe draped over the end of the bed for such eventualities.

He paused for a moment to allow his eyes to adjust to the darkness, then strode across the room and flung open the door.

A dishevelled footman, his nightshirt poking up above his waistcoat, held out a silver salver. 'This has come by express, your grace. I thought I'd better bring it up immediately.'

The nervous servant was holding a candlestick in his other hand and from the light of this Beau snapped open the wax seal.

Beau,

Mary has disappeared along with her groom and both their horses. You must come at once.

'Send word to the stables. I want my horse saddled. I'll be leaving for Town immediately.'

He yanked the bell strap that connected with his valet's room. Green would have to follow with the baggage. He wasn't going to wait.

His horse was saddled when he ran into the yard. He mounted and kicked it into a headlong gallop – there was sufficient light from the moon to make this possible. Travelling across country would be quicker but far more dangerous.

As he thundered over the fields, his horse leaping the ditches and hedges with ease, he had little time to dwell on the appalling news he had received. When he reached the city, he was obliged to slow down. This was fortuitous as his mount was exhausted after completing the journey in less than an hour.

The stable yard was busy when he trotted in, even though it was scarcely dawn. He tumbled from the saddle, tossed his reins to a waiting stable boy, and ran to the side door. Despite the early hour the place was fully illuminated.

He tossed his outer garments to a waiting footman. 'Where is Lord Aubrey?'

'In the study, your grace.'

'Have refreshments sent there immediately – two jugs of coffee and whatever is ready in the kitchen.'

Aubrey must have heard him approaching as the study door flew open before he got there. His brother's face was drawn. He appeared to have aged ten years since he had last set eyes on him.

'Thank the good Lord you are here so fast. I'm at my wits' end. We cannot talk out here – I'll explain everything inside.'

'How long has Mrs Williams been missing?'

'Since yesterday morning. She went out for her usual ride accompanied by a groom and neither of them have been seen since. We searched the park and found no sign of them – no clue that she had even been there. I then canvassed all the surrounding streets and neighbourhood, making enquiries with shopkeepers and passers-by, but to no avail.

'How can two people and two horses have vanished off the face of the earth and no one have seen it? I called in the Runners and have handed the search over to them.'

'When did you last eat, little brother?'

Aubrey rubbed his hand across his eyes and shook his head. 'I don't remember – I've not slept since the night before last.' He looked up and Beau was shocked to see tears in his brother's eyes. There was more to this than just the loss of a family friend.

'From your expression am I to understand that you have developed feelings for Mrs Williams?'

'I have and she reciprocates them, although she's doing her best to deny it. Beau, she wouldn't have left of her own volition. Someone has taken her.'

Two footmen walked in carrying laden trays. 'Put them there. We will serve ourselves.'

Once they were alone again he was free to speak. 'Have you received a ransom note? Mrs Williams…'

'Devil take it, Beau, call her Mary. If you cannot bring yourself to do that, then Cousin Mary. She will be a sister to you soon.'

'I beg your pardon, of course I shall refer to her informally. She is a wealthy woman, is she not? Someone might well have been watching her since you arrived here and has just been waiting for the opportunity to kidnap her.'

He poured them both a cup of coffee and filled a plate with an assortment of items from the tray. 'Eat this. You will feel better with food inside you. Think – has there been anything strange happen in the past three weeks?'

* * *

Aubrey didn't answer. He was weary to the bone but was determined not to rest until he had found his beloved. He sipped the coffee and the dark, aromatic brew began to revive him somewhat. He swallowed the remainder of it, leaned back in the chair and closed his eyes the better to organise his thoughts.

He went through the agonising hours he had spent looking for Mary, trying to think if there was anything anybody had said that might give him a clue as to what had happened yesterday. Was she still alive? No – he couldn't even contemplate the alternative.

Then he remembered something so obvious he had ignored its significance until now. 'If this was a normal abduction – if there is such a thing – then surely the perpetrators wouldn't have taken the horses and groom? It would have been far easier to just take her.'

'What are you suggesting?'

'I think she went along willingly. This is not what we think. Someone must have waylaid her and gave her some information that prompted her to leave the park.' He reached out and began to munch through the food on the plate beside him. With each mouthful his optimism and strength increased.

'If that's the case, why hasn't she got in touch with us? She would know you would be searching for her.'

'I haven't fathomed that part out yet. One thing I am certain of, which I wasn't until now, is that she is alive and will come back to us.' He finished his food and drank two more cups of coffee and his brother did likewise. Neither of them spoke – they were both considering the possibilities of this new information.

Beau broke the silence. 'If that's the case, and I'm not denying it seems possible, why did nobody see them?'

'I think I have been looking in the wrong places. I believe she received a note that led her to disappear before she reached the park. I made no enquiries in the opposite direction.' He heaved himself to his feet, not bothering to cover his yawn with his hand. 'I'm going to my bed for a few hours. We shall make enquiries elsewhere when I rise. By the by, Giselle and Beth are beside themselves with worry. They are determined to cancel their come-out ball if there's no word today.'

'Then we must recover Cousin Mary before they do so. I'm at a loss to understand what she could possibly have learned that engendered such dramatic action. You get some shut-eye; I shall not be far behind you.'

Aubrey spoke to the butler telling him to send the staff who had remained up to their beds. He also sent word to the outside men to begin the fresh enquiries as soon as it was light. His valet was asleep in the chair in the dressing room and he decided to leave him. He stripped off his clothes and tumbled into bed.

He was almost asleep when something that had been niggling at the corner of his mind revealed itself. He was instantly wide awake. The first day he had accompanied Mary on her early morning ride he had seen something in the bushes but dismissed it. Was it possible someone had been watching her and was just waiting for the opportunity to lure her away?

He rolled out of bed and pulled his soiled clothes back on, not bothered that his appearance would be less than pristine. He ran his fingers across his unshaven jaw – he must look like a brigand himself. He had been asleep for an hour as it was now full light.

Beau would want to hear what he'd recalled. He hammered on his brother's bedchamber door and was rewarded by a surly command to enter.

Aubrey began without preamble, ignoring the fact that he was being glared at. 'This was no opportune event. It was carefully planned and whatever instructions she was given were a lie.'

He went on to explain his reasons and now had Beau's full

attention. 'Give me a minute and I'll join you downstairs. We shall both look disreputable and be mistaken for footpads ourselves.'

Aubrey took the stairs two at a time and headed straight for the stables. He saddled Reynard himself and a groom tacked up the only other horse that would be up to his brother's weight.

The two men who were to accompany them would be obliged to ride carriage horses. Beau appeared, also unshaven, but at least he had found himself a clean shirt and fresh stock. The Duke of Silchester couldn't be seen abroad in total disarray.

'I know you are eager to begin this new search, but I think it might draw unnecessary attention to the family if we were to be seen doing it ourselves. I think we should take a closed carriage and get the grooms to do the asking whilst we remain incognito inside.'

Aubrey was about to disagree then reconsidered. 'You have a point. Also, when we find Mary we will require a carriage to bring her home. Whilst they are readying the vehicle I shall ask her abigail to pack the necessary items so she will have a change of raiment.'

'I should do something about your own appearance whilst you're up there. Being unshaven is one thing; wearing dirty clothes is quite another.'

Soon he was freshly garbed and carrying a small valise with the necessary items for Mary. The front door was standing open and he could see the carriage waiting outside. What he was surprised to observe was that the two outriders were mounted on the horses he and Beau had been going to ride.

His brother was already inside and the steps were folded up. He jumped in and settled himself opposite. 'I think she must have taken North Audley Street so we will start there. This thoroughfare leads directly to the Uxbridge Road and from there she would soon be out of the city.'

'It's the direction we take to return to Silchester Court.'

An icy lump formed in Aubrey's stomach as everything fell into place. 'It's Dunstan who has her – I'm certain of it. I met his crony, Bishop, at a posting inn behaving in a shifty way.'

He leaned out of the window and spoke to one of the outriders. 'Tell the coachman to push the horses. I want to get to the Queen's Head as soon as possible.'

'Although I'm convinced I'm correct in my assumption about Dunstan and Bishop, I cannot think of any reason why Mary would have been persuaded to leave as she did.'

'I imagine it could have been a threat to someone she was fond of, or a plea for help – again from a member of her family.'

'I don't care why she went as long as I get her back safely. I've sent my valet to obtain a special licence from Doctors' Commons. We will be wed immediately we get back to Town and the ball can be a double celebration.'

Beau stretched out his legs and sighed theatrically. 'I'm damned if I know what's wrong with this family. A little over a year ago we were jogging along quite happily together and now Bennett and Madeline are wed, Perry is a cavalry officer, and you too intend to step into parson's mousetrap as soon as you can. At this rate I shall be mouldering alone at Silchester, all my siblings having fled the family home.'

'Then I suggest that you start looking for a bride of your own. You are the oldest, you will be two and thirty on your next birthday: high time you got married.'

'I'm in no hurry to set up my nursery. I enjoy my own company and have no wish to be obliged to devote my time to another. Both Bennett and Carshalton are constantly at the beck and call of their wives. That would not do for me. I have an amiable mistress I can visit when I wish who makes no demands on me at all.'

'In which case, brother, do not bemoan the fact that you will eventually be living alone in splendour. I forgot to mention that Rushton has been a regular caller and I believe he might be interested in Giselle.'

'I thought you said he was interested in Cousin Mary. Our sister cannot marry without my consent and I would never agree to her union with someone so much older than herself. Does she reciprocate his interest?'

'I'm sure not; she and Beth are only interested in dancing and pretty gowns at the moment. They are both well aware what marriage entails – I heard them talking about the fact that both Madeline and Grace are in an interesting condition so soon after their marriages.'

'Good God! Young ladies should not discuss such matters.' Beau grinned. 'Although I must own I am delighted that the thought of childbearing puts them off marriage for the moment.' His smile faded and he sat upright on the squabs. 'You do realise you are unlikely to have children of your own if you marry Cousin Mary? She was a wife for several years without producing offspring.'

'To be honest, I should be quite content not to have a nursery full of squalling brats. We shall be able to travel once this wretched war is done. The family yacht is not used nearly often enough.'

'If I am being as frank as you on the subject of matrimony, I have no intention of marrying. I have three brothers and no doubt at least one of you will produce an heir to continue the family name.'

This was a strange conversation to be having with his older brother who was not renowned for sharing his private thoughts. 'In which case, if Bennett's child proves to be a son perhaps he should eventually move into Silchester so the boy can learn how to be the next duke.'

'My nephew can move in, but Bennett and his wife, and any other children they might have, will remain where they are.' He then closed his eyes and promptly fell asleep, leaving Aubrey alone with his thoughts.

The vehicle rocked and rattled unpleasantly owing to the speed at which they were travelling. Carriage accidents were a common occurrence and he hoped they would not be so unlucky as to be involved in one.

As it would take an hour or more to reach their destination, he thought he would catch up on his sleep too.

The outriders had gone ahead and would reach the Queen's Head long before they did and had been told to start asking the necessary questions. As he was dozing off, another unwelcome thought slipped into his mind. Mary had been away overnight without her maid in attendance. If word got out about this, her good name would be gone. This would make no difference to him, but he was very sure Beau would not be so sanguine.

Then his stomach roiled. If that bastard had forced himself upon her in the hope that he would gain himself a wealthy wife, he would not live to celebrate. He bit his lip and blinked away his tears. He loved Mary and would marry her regardless, but if the unthinkable had taken place, would she feel the same?

16

Mary hoped that they would reach Grosvenor Square before the streets became busy, as she was well aware how untidy her appearance was, and that she had mislaid her hat. She urged Cloud into a trot and the horses clattered noisily down the road – no doubt this would have been annoying to the occupants of the houses they passed, if most of them had not been set back from the thoroughfare.

After progressing for half an hour, she still did not recognise her surroundings. 'Are you quite sure you know the direction we are travelling is correct?'

Her groom reined in his gelding and she halted beside him. 'I beg your pardon, but I must have been mistaken about the church tower. I've no notion of our whereabouts. I don't reckon we're anywhere near where we should be.'

'Listen, I'm certain I heard the sound of a coachman's horn a moment ago. There must be a toll road to the east of us. We shall ride in that direction. If I'm correct then there should be a posting inn within a few miles where we can stop and ask for directions.' She glanced down at her disarray and pulled a face. 'In fact, I think if I can find somewhere salubrious, I shall request a chamber and remain there until you can fetch my maid and my necessities.'

He didn't argue with her suggestion, but then it wasn't his place to question her wishes. She hoped she had made the right decision. One thing she did know was that she didn't wish to be abroad when she was likely to be seen by passers-by.

The narrow road they took threaded between ancient buildings with scarcely room to ride side by side. After a quarter of an hour of brisk walking, they emerged into a wider route upon which there were already several carriages and diligences travelling.

'Over there, madam, where that post-chaise has just pulled out from, it's exactly what you were looking for. I can just make out the picture on the sign – I think it's a golden crown.'

'I'm not familiar with that hostelry, so I don't think we are on any thoroughfare I've travelled before.'

She pushed her horse into a collected canter and only slowed her pace as she entered the courtyard. Fortunately, there were no passengers waiting to climb on a coach. Tommy dismounted and helped her from the saddle.

'I shall go in and speak to the landlord. Good, an ostler is approaching. Make sure he takes care of Cloud, but warn him he might be bitten if he's not careful. I wish you to come in with me so it will be seen that I'm not travelling entirely alone.'

She had been mulling over exactly what she would say to explain her appearance, and the fact that she was gallivanting about the place at the crack of dawn. Inside the building was dark, little light filtering in through the leaded windows. There was a candelabra standing on a sideboard and from this she could see the place was pristine. This was a good sign.

'I see a small bell over there, Tommy, would you ring it for me? I shall remain in the shadows. You must command a room for me and say that your mistress took a tumble whilst out riding and wishes to rest until a carriage can come for her.'

The place was silent. There were no guests downstairs eating their breakfast as yet. Fate was smiling on her presently and she hoped she could escape to a private chamber before the next coach arrived.

The landlord appeared and listened to Tommy's story without showing any signs of disbelief. A maid was fetched and curtsied.

'If you'd care to come this way, madam, I will take you to a chamber. I will bring you hot water immediately. The master wants to know if you would like us to fetch a physician to examine you?'

'No, thank you, I am just shaken from my fall and have the most dreadful headache.'

Tommy was a resourceful young man and would be able to ascertain the address of the coaching inn, named the Golden Crown, and get directions to Grosvenor Square without her assistance. Neither of them carried any coins with them so she could not pay up front if she was asked to.

The room was of moderate size, but well appointed and ideal for the purpose. The maid arrived with the promised hot water.

'Would you like me to dress your hair, madam, after you have completed your ablutions? If you would care to remove the skirt of your habit I can sponge it down for you.'

Mary was about to comply then remembered she had torn off a section of her petticoat and she had no wish to display this inadequacy to anyone.

'I thank you, but there's no need. I should be grateful for some coffee, if that is available, and perhaps some toasted bread and conserve? I never break my fast until after I've ridden and think I'm feeling a little faint because of the lack of sustenance.'

The girl curtsied. 'I'll fetch it right away.'

After Mary had washed and repinned her hair she felt better. She was surprised the girl hadn't asked where she had been riding when she had taken her fall. Hopefully Tommy was already on his way to Grosvenor Square, but as she had no idea how far he would have to travel she could not be sure when rescue would arrive.

The promised tray appeared but she found her appetite had deserted her and all she could manage was a cup of coffee. The chamber overlooked the yard, which was busy now as the other guests came down. She stretched out on the bed thinking that she would sleep until Aubrey came.

Her elation at having escaped from her confinement slipped away to be replaced by a feeling of dread. She had been away from Grosvenor Square overnight, unaccompanied by her maid, and however careful the family were to keep this matter quiet, servants always gossiped.

Her throat ached and her eyes filled. She and Aubrey could never be married now whatever he might say to the contrary. His brother, the Duke of Silchester, would never accept a woman with a soiled reputation into his prestigious family.

Whatever she felt for Aubrey – and this misadventure had shown her she was deeply and irrevocably in love with him – she could not let him sacrifice himself for her sake.

* * *

When Aubrey and Beau arrived at the coaching inn it was to find the man they sought no longer resided there. Nobody they questioned had any knowledge of Dunstan and his crony.

'This is a wild goose chase, Aubrey. I'm certain Cousin Mary was not fetched here. We must return home and begin the search again from there.'

'I was so sure we would find her somewhere in this neighbourhood. If that bastard has harmed a hair of her head...'

'Whatever we feel about him, we cannot murder him in cold blood. He will be exiled and never able to return to this country.' Beau patted his shoulder as they returned to the waiting coach. 'You have my permission to teach him the error of his ways...'

'I don't need your permission to do anything; I am my own man. I have an independent income and can, and will, do as I please.'

His brother looked somewhat startled by this comment but then he understood and shook his head sadly. 'I know that you love her, little brother, but the situation is untenable. When word of this gets out, and believe me it will eventually, she will be *persona non grata* in society.'

Aubrey rudely interrupted him. 'I don't give a damn for your views or those of society. Whatever took place, I will marry Mary and you cannot stop me. If you will not accept her into the family, then so be it, I can live without your company.' He paused in his tirade before he could say something he regretted. He had no wish to exacerbate matters further.

His brother was silent and Aubrey spoke again, this time less intemperately. 'I have no wish to be at daggers drawn with you. I should be devastated to be obliged to give up any contact with you, my brothers and sisters. However, I love Mary and she loves me, and whatever the circumstances we will be together. I just pray that in time you can accept this.'

For some reason Beau didn't argue, he merely shrugged. 'Whatever you decide, I will support you as will the rest of the family. Being ostracised, being unable to visit your clubs, attend parties, send your children to the best educational establishments, might not seem important to you now, but... well... we shall talk no more of this at the moment. I've been travelling all night; forgive me if I get some shut-eye.'

The carriage lapsed into silence, leaving Aubrey to consider what had been said. He wouldn't dwell on what might have happened, what might be said, but concentrate on finding his beloved. Whatever Beau said to the contrary, when he eventually caught up with Dunstan he would kill him and take the consequences.

Mary was a resourceful, courageous and intelligent woman – not a shy, young debutante. He had every faith in her, that she would survive and return to him. It might take a while to convince her he was unbothered by the loss of her reputation, but he was confident he would succeed in the end.

He was roused from his doze when the carriage rocked to a sudden halt and someone hammered on the door. His brother was there before him and lowered the window. Staring in at them was the groom who always accompanied Mary on her rides.

'Your grace, my lord, Mrs Williams is safe and unharmed. I was on my way to find you. If you would care to turn the carriage and follow me I will lead you directly to her.'

'Where is she?' Aubrey said.

'At the Golden Crown, a decent coaching inn a few miles from here.'

Aubrey beckoned to one of the outriders. 'Return to Grosvenor Square and let them know we have located Mrs Williams and will be returning with her soon.'

Even as he was finishing his sentence their coachman was beginning his manoeuvre despite the angry shouts and blasts of the horns from the other coachmen that accompanied it.

The horses would be tired after travelling so far and so fast, but they could rest as long as was needed once he was at Mary's side. The carriage was eventually facing in the correct direction and moved off.

'Thank God she is safe. I care not for the opinion of others, Beau; the only thing that matters is that you and I, and the rest of the family, know she has come out of this unscathed.'

His brother returned his smile but he could not help but notice Beau was not as delighted as he was. Time enough to smooth things over with his brother once his darling was safely back beside him.

'I wonder how she came to be at this place. Did she escape? Did her captors leave her there for us to find?'

'No doubt all will be explained to us in due course, little brother. At least we have the requisites she will need to restore her appearance. Don't do anything precipitous; if you push matters she will refuse you.'

'I must tell her that nothing has changed as far as I'm concerned, that I have a special licence on its way and we can be married immediately. Once she is safely part of the Silchester clan I defy anyone to speak ill of her.'

'That's as may be, Aubrey. I know that you will do as you want regardless of my opinion, but stop to think a little. She has had an unpleasant and frightening experience – do you really think she will be ready to jump into your arms and your bed so soon? Remember, she was happily married for several years to a man considerably older than her and has been left a wealthy widow.'

* * *

Mary eventually fell into a light sleep but her dreams were unpleasant and she jerked awake after an hour or so. She had removed the skirt of her riding habit and draped it over a chair whilst she rested and she quickly tied this back on.

She splashed her face with water and used the brush thoughtfully provided by the maid to tidy her hair. Satisfied she looked as well as could be expected in the circumstances she went to the window to watch the comings and goings in the yard.

Tommy turned in from the road followed immediately by a carriage that she recognised. She watched Aubrey and his brother clamber out and stepped hurriedly away from the window. She had not expected the duke to be there and this would make what she had to say far more difficult.

There was barely a moment to compose herself before the door burst open and Aubrey appeared. He tossed a valise onto the bed and then snatched her from her feet. He covered her face with kisses, murmuring loving words of reassurance and her decision to terminate the relationship was left unspoken.

'My darling, I cannot tell you how happy I am to see you. I have been beside myself past few hours. Tell me what transpired.'

He had replaced her on her feet and was leading her to the *chaise longue* in order to continue the conversation. She looked nervously at the door, expecting the duke to join them.

'I saw your brother get out of the carriage. Are we to expect him too?'

'He cannot join us here; you have no sitting room. By rights I should not be here either, but as I consider you my future wife, I refuse to be bound by propriety.'

Now was the time to tell him she could never marry him, that he would be ostracised by his friends if they were to be united. Instead, she said something else entirely.

'You have not asked me formally, my love, and must not do so until you have heard my sorry tale.' Quickly she explained what had happened and how she had managed to escape.

'I have men searching for him. He will be found and I will deal with him...'

'You must give me your word, Aubrey, that you will not murder him. It will be you who faces the gallows if you do so. Your pedigree will not prevent the law extracting due process.'

'Beau has already said the same, so don't fret, sweetheart. I shall not kill him even though that is what I would like to do.'

'I was surprised to see your brother with you. I doubt that he will sanction any union between us after this. Although we know that nothing untoward took place whilst I was away, Dunstan can spread whatever malicious gossip he wishes and people will believe it. My absence will have been noted by the servants and they will have spoken about it.'

He took her hands and raised them to his mouth; her heart skipped a beat and she was unaccountably short of breath. Much as she had loved her dearest Freddie, *his* touch had never produced such tumultuous feelings.

'My darling girl, I care not for what others say. My brother agrees – if we wish to marry then we have his blessing. I love you and cannot live without you.' He dropped to one knee without releasing his hold. 'Marry me, sweetheart; make me the happiest of men. I have acquired a special licence and we can tie the knot as soon as we return to Grosvenor Square.'

She knew she should refuse him for both their sakes; that whatever his feelings on the subject at present he would regret the marriage when he found himself unable to visit his clubs, or be included in invitations to the best houses in the country.

'I will marry you, my love, but not in such a havey-cavey fashion. If we get married it will be with our families present and in your chapel at Silchester Court when the Season is over. I would prefer it if we do not make any formal announcement until after the ball. I have no wish to overshadow this event for Giselle or Beth.'

He rejoined her on the daybed. 'Waiting until June to have

you in my bed will be an almost impossible task – but for you, I shall endure it. As long as I know that in a few weeks you will be mine, I will be content.'

They were interrupted by a polite tap on the door. The maid who had been taking care of her stepped in and curtsied. 'The gentleman has asked if you are ready to depart, madam. He is getting fresh horses from our stable.'

Aubrey answered for her. 'We shall be down directly.'

'If Tommy rides Cloud then his mount can rest and be collected with your team.'

He agreed this was a sensible idea but did not solve the puzzle of how the Silchester mounts would find their way home. No doubt a bevy of grooms would be sent to lead them back.

She wasn't looking forward to being closeted with the duke on the return journey. However, when she was newly gowned and wearing a bonnet she would feel more ready to face him.

'It will take me but a few minutes to change my apparel, my dear; you must wait for me downstairs. Thank you for remembering to bring a fresh ensemble.'

It took her far longer than she'd intended to change. Half an hour passed before she was satisfied with her appearance. The chip straw bonnet had a deep brim, which hid her face. Her muslin gown and matching spencer fortunately covered her riding boots. Jessie had not thought to include suitable footwear.

Downstairs she was greeted by the duke. He bowed. 'I am pleased to see you looking so well, cousin.' His smile was warm as he continued. 'Might I be the first to congratulate you on your betrothal to my brother? I understand and applaud your decision to keep the information within the family for the moment.'

She dipped. 'Thank you, sir, and I apologise for keeping you waiting.'

'As it happens I am glad that you did, my dear. We no longer need to borrow a team as ours are now sufficiently rested. I shall ride your horse myself.'

He offered his arm and she took it. If she told him that Cloud might attempt to unseat him it might seem as if she doubted his prowess as a horseman. Tommy was well aware of her gelding's dislike of men and would surely warn him?

As the carriage pulled away something occurred to her – the duke would either have to ride bareback or use her saddle.

17

Beau waited until his brother and his future sister-in-law were safely installed in the carriage before finding his own mount. Mary's groom had already departed and for some reason the courtyard was suddenly devoid of ostlers. This meant he would have to fetch the grey gelding for himself – not something he was pleased to do.

A stable lad gestured towards the end stall. 'That varmint won't let no one near him, mister, so he's not ready for the lady.'

God's teeth! Why hadn't Mary spoken up? He could hardly use her saddle and he had no wish to travel the five miles without one. When he approached the gelding, his ears went back and he bared his teeth – hardly a friendly greeting.

He remained a safe distance from the animal, making no attempt to touch him. He spoke to the boy without turning his head. 'I shall need to buy a saddle. Do you have something that will fit this beast?'

'I reckon we do. I'll fetch it.'

The horse continued to snap at him and his hoofs drummed against the rear of his stall. Perhaps it might be wiser to borrow a nag and lead the grey. No – he had never been defeated by a horse and this one would be no exception.

'Here you are, mister; it ain't perfect, but I reckon it will be a good fit. The master said it were a guinea.'

This was exorbitant for the dilapidated saddle he was handed but he had no choice if he wished to be able to return home immediately.

He removed the bridle from a hook and walked to the stall and grabbed the animal's top lip before he could attack. Once the bit was in his mouth it would be far easier to control him. He led him outside and tethered him to a metal ring so the animal was unable to swing his head from side to side. This still left him free to lash out with his hoofs and Beau was relieved to have got the saddle on and the girth tightened without being kicked.

It would be too dangerous to take the horse to the mounting block, so he would vault onto his back and then get the boy to untie the rope. He rammed his feet into the stirrups, threw a coin to the lad, gathered up the reins and was ready.

The gelding was ominously still, but his every muscle was taut. As soon as he was released he would do his best to unseat his rider. Falling from a bucking horse onto cobbles could prove a painful and possibly fatal experience – it was one he didn't intend to have.

'Untie him now and stand clear.'

The animal erupted beneath him almost pitching him head first to the ground. Beau had his hand wound firmly into the wiry mane, his knees rock hard against the saddle and his feet firmly in the irons. He would not be thrown unless the horse lost his footing.

His teeth were being jarred in his head and with every buck a shockwave travelled up his spine. Somehow he retained sufficient control to force his mount to leave the courtyard and enter the main thoroughfare. Here there was more room and if he could keep them out of the way of any passing vehicles they should not come to grief.

This performance continued for a further few minutes but then the bucking stopped and the gelding tried to reach round and take lumps out of his leg. After trying this twice more, his antics ceased. Beau felt the horse's muscles relax and to his astonishment he found himself astride a compliant horse.

'Well done, old fellow, we should deal splendidly together from now on.' The horse flicked his ears back and forth a few times and then responded willingly enough. After half a mile there was a gap in the hedge and Beau guided him through.

'I think a good gallop will settle your fidgets.' He sat deep in the saddle and gave the horse the signal to canter. Then he slackened the reins and squeezed again – the grey moved smoothly into a gallop and they raced across the fields in perfect harmony. They jumped half a dozen hedges and as many ditches and when Beau asked him to stop the horse responded immediately.

'You are a magnificent beast, far too powerful to be a lady's ride. I shall find Mary something more suitable.'

The speed they had been travelling meant that even when he rejoined the road, he was well ahead of the carriage and arrived at Grosvenor Square in advance of the others.

He was somewhat surprised by the reaction of the grooms to his appearance but assumed it was the fact that he was riding Mary's horse.

'The carriage is not far behind me. Take care of this animal – he has been ridden hard.'

* * *

Aubrey put his arm around Mary's waist as soon as she was settled comfortably beside him on the squabs. She relaxed against him, resting her head on his shoulder as if it belonged there.

'My darling, I cannot tell you how happy I am to have you here beside me safe and well. Beau is... Good God! Did you think to warn him that your horse hates all men?'

She sighed. 'I did not, my love, but I'm certain Cloud would not have the temerity to behave badly with a duke on his back.'

'And I suppose you are comfortable with the thought that he only has a side-saddle upon which to sit?'

'Your brother is a resourceful man; he will resolve the problem without too much difficulty.' She put her feet up on the seat then leaned back so that she was cradled in his arms in a most delightful fashion. 'Are we to tell the girls of our betrothal? What about my mama? I should like to let her know as it will take her several weeks to get herself sufficiently organised to travel to Silchester. She dislikes leaving her home but I'm hoping she will make an exception for our wedding.'

'Once the ball is over perhaps we could visit her together? My brother will be in charge and I'm certain Lady Johnson will be happy to take over your duties for a week or so.'

'I should like that – thank you for suggesting it. I still can't quite comprehend that we are to make a match of it. Freddie was twenty years my senior and you are three years my junior. Good gracious, that means he could have been your father.'

He tilted her face and kissed her before answering. 'He could have been yours too. I will make you happy, sweetheart. I promise you will never regret agreeing to be my wife.'

'And if we never have a family of our own? Will you still feel the same?'

'I'm not overfond of children and, if I am honest, I would

prefer to have you to myself. Also childbearing can be a dangerous occupation and I would be in terror of losing you.'

He couldn't see her expression as she had turned her face into his shoulder but her response was reassuring. 'Then I shall stop worrying about this. Forgive me, I have slept little over the past twenty-four hours and would dearly like to rest now.'

She had removed her fetching bonnet and discarded it on the other seat. This gave him access to her hair and he was sorely tempted to remove the pins and run his fingers through its shiny length. He thought better of this as she needed to look respectable when they arrived.

He stretched out his feet and closed his eyes; if she had had little sleep last night, he had had none. He didn't wake until the carriage slowed its progress in order to turn under the archway that led to the turning circle at the rear of the house.

He gently shook her shoulder. 'We are here, Mary. I'm sure you wish to put your bonnet back on before we descend.'

Slowly she sat. Her smile was radiant; she looked even more beautiful than she had before – if that were possible. 'I feel so much better after my sleep.' He stretched out and retrieved her bonnet before putting it back in place. She expertly tied the bows, shook out the folds in her gown, and gave him another heart-stopping smile.

'Do I look quite respectable, Aubrey, my love? We did not discuss exactly how much we should tell the girls about my abduction – I thought I would just tell them I was locked into a comfortable room and released first thing this morning. I shall not mention Dunstan, or the fact that I was obliged to climb out of the window.'

'That will be more than enough. Can you remember if we have a social engagement this evening?'

'I'm certain we do not. The ball is tomorrow night and we will all wish to be fresh for that.'

The under-coachman opened the door and let down the steps. Aubrey stepped down first and then turned to hand her down.

'I do believe I can hear my horse cavorting in his stall. I'm so glad your brother arrived here with no mishap.'

'Not as glad as I, Cousin Mary. I believe that you neglected to mention the fact your horse objects to having anyone else on his back.' Beau was leaning casually against the wall, his expression serious but his eyes laughing.

'I know, it was most remiss of me. You obviously had no difficulty, so there was no harm done.'

Beau smiled. 'He did his best to kill me. When he failed to do so we came to an understanding.' All might have been well if he had not continued. 'He is not a mount for a lady. I shall find you something I think will suit you better.'

She stiffened and her eyes flashed dangerously. His brother did not see the warning sign and continued to pour oil on the fire.

'Cloud will make an excellent addition to my stable.' He pushed himself away from the wall and was about to stroll away when she stopped him.

'Your grace, you are forgetting a pertinent fact. The horse belongs to me and I do not intend to relinquish him to you or anybody else. I shall continue to ride him when I wish to.' She stared at him and his brother's friendly demeanour was replaced by a glacial expression.

'In which case, madam, I shall say no more on the matter.' Beau nodded and strode off in high dudgeon.

* * *

Mary regretted speaking her mind – the last thing she wished to do was cause offence to her host. 'I should not have said that. I must go after him and put matters right between us.' She was about to dash off when Aubrey restrained her.

'No, my love, don't go now. My brother will realise his suggestion was high-handed and come to you when he has recovered his temper.'

'In which case, I shall be guided by you.' There was no time for her to continue as Beth and Giselle hurtled down the passage and threw their arms around her.

'We are so pleased to see you back. We have been beside ourselves with worry. You look as though you have been visiting a friend, not a hair out of place. How can that be?' Beth said as she stepped away, wiping her eyes on her sleeve like a child.

Giselle seemed incapable of speech and reluctant to release her. 'Dearest girls, I am so pleased to be home. Shall we go inside where I can tell you what transpired and who was the perpetrator of this outrage?'

Once in the privacy of the drawing room she gave them the edited version of events and they exclaimed and clapped their hands, and shook their heads in turn. 'So you see, my dears, that horrible man will not achieve his ends. Aubrey and I are betrothed and he will get his comeuppance as soon as he is found.'

'He must be touched in the attic,' Beth said, 'to go to such lengths just because you offended him.'

'He was excluded from all the best parties, blackballed from his club. For some gentlemen that would be something they could not live with.' Aubrey took her hand and pulled her gently to her feet. 'You have yet to remove your bonnet and spencer, my love. I suggest you retire to your apartment where your maid can help you do so.'

She was about to protest that she was quite capable of removing them herself then reconsidered. She was in need of a bath after being kept in such unpleasant conditions overnight. 'I shall do so immediately. Don't look so concerned, girls; I should not be gone above an hour. I'm sure there are several things we need to discuss about the arrangements for your ball tomorrow night.'

They were reluctant to part with her, but she insisted. Aubrey accompanied her upstairs. 'I have ordered a bath for you, sweetheart. I'm sure you will wish to wash away the last remnants of your captivity. I intend to change my garments, shave, and will be downstairs as soon as I'm done.'

Without thinking she reached out and touched his face. 'I quite like the way you look, my love; it gives you a piratical air.'

They parted with only a smile when she would have much preferred to exchange an embrace. If they were to wait until June to marry, then she must repress her lustful thoughts. Knowing what was involved when a husband and wife shared the marriage bed made the anticipation so much keener.

Jessie asked no questions, but was obviously delighted to have her mistress safely home. After a soak in a lemon-scented bath, her hair freshly washed, Mary felt fully restored.

'Put out something pretty, preferably a gown I've not worn before. I want to look my best.'

'I have the Indian muslin ready for you, madam. It's the height of fashion and the colour is perfect on you.'

The girl held it up whilst Mary was drying herself. 'Daffodil yellow and cream stripes are most unusual; I had quite forgotten I'd purchased this material. I believe it has matching slippers, does it not?'

'I have them here, madam. There is a parasol, reticule and

bonnet lined with the same stuff but I don't suppose you will require them today.'

In less than the allotted time Mary was on her way down to join the girls, and hopefully her future husband, in the drawing room for midday refreshments. She had been tense, expecting to be treated differently, receive surreptitious looks from the staff, but things were as they had been before. It was as if she had not been abducted at all.

She was about to descend when Aubrey called her name. His voice echoed around the gallery and must have been quite audible to the footmen who stood sentinel in the entrance hall. He arrived at her side in a rush.

'Darling girl, you look quite delicious in that gown.' He inhaled her scent. 'And you smell even better.'

She couldn't restrain her laugh. 'I believe you are suggesting I smelt less than pleasant before. My hair is not dry, which is why I got my maid to braid it. Do you like the coronet?'

He bent his head so he could whisper in her ear. The touch of his warm breath sent her pulse racing. 'I would much prefer to see it loose, my love.'

'And so you shall, but not until we are wed.' She moved a safe distance from him. 'I have written to my mother – not to tell her about what happened – but that I am engaged to you.'

'Beau will have done the same for Bennett and Madeline. I cannot wait to be able to celebrate in style.'

'You can put a notice in *The Times* when we have settled on a date for our nuptials, but until then we have agreed to keep the information within the family.'

The girls were in the drawing room excitedly examining a pile of invitations that had arrived that morning. 'If we accept all of these, Mary, we shall be out every night until we leave,' Giselle said.

'Then we must be circumspect in our choices. We do not have the stamina to survive such a regime of socialising and partying.'

Aubrey had remained at the door. 'Excuse me, ladies, I must speak to my brother. We shall join you when luncheon is served.'

Beth seemed unbothered by recent events and was as sunny-natured as always; however, Giselle was subdued. Mary drew her to one side. 'Shall we leave your cousin to sort the cards into piles? I wish to speak to you privately.'

As they were using the drawing room there was plenty of room to stroll around at the far end without being overheard by Beth, who was engrossed in her task and didn't comment on their perambulations.

'Tell me, Giselle, why are you so quiet?'

'I'm beginning to believe that this family is cursed and blessed in equal measures. In less than two years we have had accidents, shootings, midnight elopements, attempted murders and now an abduction. Admittedly we have also had two marriages, one betrothal, and are expecting two happy events in the autumn.'

Mary was somewhat startled by this information. It took a full half an hour for the girl to explain the events to which she was referring. When she had done with her exciting tale Giselle wrung her hands.

'So you see, Mary, why I am concerned. I fear that for every happy event the family experiences, we also suffer a catastrophe.'

18

Aubrey found his brother reading the newspaper in the study. Beau had changed his apparel too and was once more the immaculate gentleman he was accustomed to see. He seemed unsurprised to see him.

'I was expecting you. Have you come to reprimand me for trying to steal Cousin Mary's horse?'

'I'm sure you have realised the error of your ways. I hope you are not anticipating an apology from her?'

His brother chuckled. 'I believe it is I who must apologise, not her. She is a remarkable woman; the more I get to know her, the better I like her. She will make you an admirable partner.'

'Indeed, she will. Mary is an unconventional bride – but she is perfect for me. Life will certainly not be dull when married to her.' He flopped down on the leather sofa. 'Actually, I came to speak to you about that bastard who abducted her.'

'I have a dozen excellent men searching for him. I know you wish to mete out justice yourself, but it is better left to the professionals. He will be dealt with severely, and put on a ship to the colonies. His pernicious presence will not bother this family again.'

'In which case I shall try and put these past two days behind me. I wish my twin could get furlough and stand up for me at my wedding, but I suppose fighting for King and Country must take precedence. Have you had word from him recently?'

'Nothing for a few weeks. I'm certain we would hear soon enough if anything had occurred.'

'He is my other half; I would know if he was in trouble long before any letter reached here. I'm not worried about his safety, just curious about his adventures as a cavalry officer.'

'I think he is invaluable to his regiment because of his facility with languages. I'm surprised that you are not as fluent in French or Spanish as he is.'

'We might be identical in appearance, but we have different interests. I take it you've written to the others with my good news.'

'I have. I have also put in motion plans for your wedding at the end of June. We shall have a garden party with the tenants and staff as we did for Bennett and Grace's wedding, and hold a ball for our friends and neighbours.'

Aubrey frowned. 'I think that was unwise of you, brother; such matters are best left to the bride to decide.'

'If she is marrying into my family then she will have to learn to follow the rules that govern it. Silchester weddings are always held at the Court.'

'That's fustian and you know it, Beau. Madeline married Carshalton in that doctor's house. I have a special licence in my bureau upstairs and we can be married wherever we wish.'

His brother raised his hands in surrender. 'You are quite correct, but I should be honoured if you and Mary would consent to tie the knot at home with your family present.'

The fact that his brother had dropped the word *cousin* when talking of his future wife was a good sign. 'We have agreed not to discuss anything to do with the wedding until after the ball. Which reminds me, is everything in place?'

'I've no idea, and little interest in the subject. I keep excellent staff and it is their role to see that matters run smoothly.' They were interrupted by a knock on the door and a footman politely announced that refreshments were now being served in the small dining room.

Mary and the girls were already there and were busy helping themselves from the buffet set out on the sideboard for their delectation.

'Aubrey, your grace, we were beginning to think you were not joining us,' Mary said.

Beau strolled over to her. 'I must apologise for overstepping the mark, Mary. I am a duke, you know, and expect to have my own way at all times.'

'I have been considering your suggestion, and although I'm not going to give up my horse, you are welcome to ride him whenever you want.' She half-smiled and Aubrey held his breath, waiting for her to say something provoking. 'Are we now on more familiar terms? Dare I use your given name as you have just used mine?'

'I would prefer not to be addressed so formally. My family call me Beau and I would like you to do so.' His smile was warm as he continued. 'I shall certainly take you up on your kind offer. Cloud is a magnificent animal.'

'He is indeed, but I can assure you that he has never let a man on his back before. He was cruelly treated in his previous home and developed an aversion to all gentlemen.'

The remainder of the meal was spent discussing the invitations that the girls had selected. Aubrey barely followed this conversation; he preferred to watch the woman he loved as she laughed, talked and waved her hands about.

He had not been looking for a bride, had not expected to fall in love, but here he was about to enter parson's mousetrap and it could not come soon enough for him.

* * *

Mary abandoned her morning ride. Somehow the prospect of being out in the park so early no longer appealed. She would leave it for a day or two and allow the duke to exercise her horse. Today would be given over to supervising the final preparations for the ball tonight. There was to be no dinner beforehand with chosen guests as was often the custom. They were to have trays in their own rooms, which meant they did not have to be ready until nine o'clock when the first guests would start to arrive.

The flowers had been arranged yesterday and were now being positioned according to her plan. The colour scheme had been selected to complement the gowns the girls were wearing, and ribbons matching these colours had been tied around the vases.

Aubrey found her straightening one of the bows on a magnificent arrangement that would be positioned in the entrance hall.

'Sweetheart, you should leave this to the staff. They are quite capable of carrying out orders and it doesn't require you to be personally involved.'

'I'm sure it doesn't, my love, but I am used to being active. We need to talk, and I am ready for a walk around the garden. Would you care to join me?'

They left via the open French doors at the far end of the ballroom, which led directly onto the terrace. 'I have had lanterns positioned in the garden; also, there will be flambeaux out here so couples can walk about if they become overheated inside. You will note, my love, that there are no dark corners where inappropriate behaviour could take place.'

'You have thought of everything; your organisational skills are second to none. It must be because you were once a soldier's wife.'

This was the opening she wanted. She pointed to a stone bench tucked away beneath an arbour of honeysuckle and rose. 'Shall we sit there for a while?'

Once they were comfortably settled, she took his hands in hers. 'You need to know a little about my past. I have said more than once that I was happily married, and that was the truth. I loved Freddie, but if I'm honest, I believe I loved being the wife of the colonel more than I loved him. I married him because he could offer me a life of excitement and an opportunity to see the world.'

He looked unsurprised by this information and, emboldened by his expression, she continued. 'I was glad we didn't have children as that would have meant I had to return to England. What I'm trying to say, my dear, is that I am not a conventional woman. I have no wish to be cloistered and protected, to spend my days on doing useless embroidery, abysmal watercolours and raising a family.'

She risked a glance and was delighted to see he was amused by her revelations rather than shocked.

'My darling, I don't believe I would have fallen in love with you if you had been like other women. It is impossible to travel on the Continent at the moment because of the wretched war, but we could go to India, or the colonies, go wherever you might wish. There is a yacht moored somewhere or other belonging to the family that is scarcely used. What say you to taking that on a trip around the world?'

'I should love that above anything; I have made ocean journeys several times and well remember the cramped conditions and lack of facilities. Will there be sufficient room to take Jessie and your valet?'

'The vessel was built to accommodate a retinue of servants; the state cabin that we will occupy is more than large enough. We should certainly take our personal attendants, and one or two others besides. What we cannot take are horses – they do not travel well.'

'You must ask your brother's permission before we sail away, possibly for years, in his yacht. I wish now we were getting married sooner...'

His eyes darkened as he deliberately misunderstood her comment. Before she could protest she was sitting on his lap and she forgot everything except the pleasure of his mouth on hers. Fortunately, common sense asserted itself before things got quite out of hand.

'Release me, my love. We cannot be seen to be making love in so public a place.'

Again, he teased her. 'Then shall we go somewhere private and continue this to its conclusion?'

She jumped to her feet and tried to look cross. 'We shall not; we shall continue on our walk like a respectable couple. I have no wish to pre-empt our wedding night – no, that's not correct; I should love to share my bed with you – but we will not do so. It would be disrespectful to your brother and set a poor example to the girls.'

His roar of laughter sent a flock of sparrows circling noisily into the air. 'I was not intending to invite them to watch, sweetheart, and I can assure you that no one would be aware of what we did,' he said between his splutters of amusement.

She was tempted to kick him smartly on the shins but reconsidered as she was wearing her indoor slippers. 'You are quite impossible, sir. I am going inside where I shall find more sensible company.'

He waved a nonchalant hand but made no effort to join her. It was her turn to laugh. He was unable to move because his embarrassment would be visible – he was now obliged to remain on the bench, with his coat-tails placed strategically across his lap, until matters rectified themselves.

The remainder of the day was spent overseeing the final details for the ball. Aubrey and the duke failed to join them for midday refreshments and she wondered what had detained them. No doubt she would hear all about it when they met up later.

* * *

Aubrey remained in the garden until he was recovered and then went in search of his brother. As expected, Beau was in his study.

'Excellent, I wish to speak to you. I've just heard news of Dunstan.'

'Has he been apprehended?'

'No, he left the country on a ship for the Indies the same day that Mary was abducted. He obviously had no intention of returning to the house after he had spoken to her. This was carefully planned. I believe that he's left confident in the belief that he has achieved his aim – that of ruining her reputation, making it impossible for the two of you to find happiness together.'

'Dammit! He has escaped justice...'

'His actions have obliged him to exile himself from England. He will never be able to return and will eventually learn that his machinations failed and he has sacrificed his estates for nothing.'

'Then I suppose I must be satisfied. The man's fit for Bedlam, if you want my opinion; no sane man would have reacted the way he did.' He found himself a seat and broached the matter about which he had come to speak to his brother.

'I would like to borrow your yacht for a year or two. Mary and I wish to spend our time visiting exotic places, and the best way to do this is within the comfort of a private vessel.'

'I shall give it to you as your wedding gift on the understanding that you will loan it to any other member of the family when you eventually return to these shores.'

'That is a generous gift indeed. We might be away for some years, but will be happy to make it available to any of our siblings after that.'

'It is in good shape, was recently refurbished, but at the moment has a skeleton crew. If you wish to use it in a few weeks you must go down and supervise any changes you might need; set in motion the hiring of a crew and make sure the yacht is provisioned to your satisfaction.'

'I know very little about seafaring. Could I not prevail upon you to accompany me? I want it to be perfect and that means having experienced sailors and a knowledgeable captain. I must also arrange for sufficient gold to be stowed somewhere on board. I have no wish to stint on my extended trip.'

'This must be set in motion as soon as possible, Aubrey. I should be happy to go with you as soon as this ball is over. I'm sure Mary and the girls will be able to manage for a few days without either of us here.'

'I haven't spoken to her yet about the arrangements for our wedding. As this is to take place in less than eight weeks, things must be put in hand immediately. I'm going to suggest all of them go back to Silchester, not remain in London whilst we are absent.'

His brother raised an eyebrow. 'Good luck with that, little brother. Mary might be happy to oblige, but I cannot see the girls wishing to abandon any of the invitations they have accepted.'

'I shall speak to them myself. I suppose that if they won't go, then instructions can be sent by letter. At least we do not have to have the banns read – we can use the special licence I have already obtained.'

Beau stood up. 'I am walking round to our club. Why don't you join me? The exercise and fresh air will do us both good.'

'I should prefer to ride. Why don't we make an excursion to the park; I should like to see how you handle Silver Cloud.'

On their return, after a pleasant and uneventful ride, he went in search of Mary only to be told she had retired to her apartment. He rapped on her sitting room door and she answered his knock herself.

'Come in, my love. I have missed you today.' She had not yet begun her elaborate preparations for the ball as she was still wearing a delightful dimity gown.

He didn't close the door behind him. They might be betrothed but they must still not break too many rules. 'I have much to tell you. Do you have time to hear it now or are you about to get ready for this evening?'

'Good heavens, it will take me no more than an hour to prepare and it's not yet five o'clock. I am expecting my dinner to arrive at any moment. Do you wish to dine with me?'

'I do indeed. I shall have my own tray redirected. I see that your maid has already set up a table by the window. Shall we sit there?'

He had no wish to discuss anything pertaining to the Dunstan matter until he could be sure they were not going to be overheard.

'I gather that your brother went out on my horse. Did Cloud behave himself?'

'He tried to take a lump or two from me but appeared

delighted to see Beau. You can be sure he will be well looked after when we are away on our travels.'

'I am looking forward to this evening. I intend to dance as often as I'm asked but will, of course, reserve the first and the supper dance for you.'

'As we are now betrothed we can dance together as often as we wish.' He wasn't happy with the idea that she might spend time with other gentlemen tonight.

'Remember, my love, we are keeping this information inside the family at the moment. I must not appear to favour you above any other partner. You must dance with both Giselle and Beth. No doubt I shall be obliged to stand up with the duke.'

Her lack of enthusiasm for this treat made him smile. 'I can hear the food arriving. I'm hungry as I didn't take luncheon today.'

The footmen didn't remain to serve; they merely placed the dishes, crockery and cutlery on the table and departed as quietly as they had arrived, leaving them to talk in privacy.

19

Mary wasn't sure if she was relieved or angry that the man who had abducted her was now out of reach of justice. 'Then let us hope the matter is at an end and we can safely forget about it. There is one thing that I'm curious about – what happened to his friend? I forget his name.'

'He too has vanished, although I admit we have not been actively searching for him. He doesn't seem to have been involved with this particular venture.'

'It still seems rather strange that they attempted to attract the interest of our girls. One would have thought they might have tried on the fringes of society – they would have had more success there.'

'That has puzzled me as well, sweetheart. Shall we talk of happier things? What do you think about my news that Beau has given me his yacht?'

'It is a most generous wedding gift. I hope you will not be offended, but I must ask if you would like me to transfer funds so you can get everything prepared for our departure. I know what I have will become yours, but...'

'I was going to ask you if you would do so, but as always, you have read my mind. How do you feel about spending the next week away from here whilst my brother and I attend to matters at Rye?'

'I should like it above everything, but I doubt the girls will acquiesce so easily. I shall ask Lady Johnson if she would be prepared to step in as chaperone in my absence.'

'Why don't you suggest she and her progeny move into Silchester House? There is ample room and she might rather enjoy residing here.'

'Are you sure your brother will not object?'

'I'm certain he will think it's an excellent idea.' He covered her hand with his own and his eyes were warm as he spoke. 'I admit I will be happier if you are not gallivanting about Town in my absence. I have no wish for a predatory gentleman to entice you away from me.'

'There is no danger of that. I love you and no one else is of any interest. I shall write a note immediately to Lady Johnson issuing the invitation. This means she can give us her answer when she comes this evening.'

She shook out the crumbs from her skirt. 'I am replete. There is another thing I meant to tell you, my love. Beth and Giselle have assured me they have met no one they wish to become better acquainted with. They are loving every minute of their time here and intend to come back next year and repeat the process. Neither of them are in any hurry to get married.'

'Beau will be pleased to hear that. I think he is rather dreading being obliged to occupy that vast place on his own. Although both girls are considered old enough to set up their own establishment, I too am pleased they wish to remain single for a while longer.'

They embraced briefly and then he strolled off to his own

chambers whilst she wrote the letter to Lady Johnson. The thought of being able to spend a week away from Grosvenor Square filled her with joy. This was the one area in which Aubrey and she were different. He loved the rush and bustle of the city whilst she much preferred to be in the peace and tranquillity of the countryside. That is, if she could not be dashing about on the Continent.

She would go to her own estates, those left to her by dearest Freddie, and make sure her affairs were in order before everything was handed over to Aubrey's control. It was a little further to Suffolk, where they were situated, than it was to Silchester, but the journey was still possible to achieve in less than a day. Of course, if Lady Johnson was not agreeable to this arrangement then she must remain where she was.

The note was written and sent down to be delivered by a footman. Hanover Square was not far from here, and she had asked for whoever delivered it to wait for a reply. It would be so much easier if she had a response before the ball began so she could arrange things for an early departure.

* * *

Jessie clapped her hands and stood back in admiration. 'You look like a princess, madam. You will be the most beautiful lady at the ball tonight.'

Her maid was somewhat biased but Mary had to admit she had never looked better. She was wearing an emerald parure, another gift from her previous husband, and it certainly added to her ensemble. Her ball gown was of the palest green silk, with exquisite emerald roses around the low neckline, around the hem and even on her matching evening slippers.

'I'm glad I have the necklace to wear as I'm not comfortable exposing so much of my bosom.' She had promised to oversee the girls' final preparations and was already somewhat tardy.

'There is no need for you to wait up, Jessie; I can step out of this gown without your assistance.' She was about to leave when the reply arrived from Lady Johnson stating she would be delighted to take over the responsibility of chaperoning the girls and even more thrilled to be able to do so from Silchester House.

'I am going to spend the week in Suffolk. Please pack my trunk and send a message to the stables that I wish to depart tomorrow.'

* * *

Aubrey had been listening for the sound of Mary's sitting room door, which would indicate she was on her way to join the girls in their apartment. He wanted to be the first to view her in her finery. He was not disappointed. She was the most beautiful young woman in the kingdom – he could hardly comprehend that she had chosen him to be her second husband.

'You look lovely, sweetheart. I shall have to stand scowling behind you all evening to keep hopeful partners at bay. Indeed, I think I might ask my brother to stand and glower beside me to ensure you are not stolen away.'

'You are ridiculous, my love. Do you not know me well enough by now to understand that I can discourage unwanted gentlemen myself?' She moved gracefully towards him and stood on her toes to kiss him.

It took all his control not to sweep her off her feet. Somehow, he managed to reciprocate her gentle gesture. 'Do you think I might be allowed to see the girls or must I linger outside until they are ready to descend?'

'They will be delighted to see you. This is a big day for both of them – I never had such an occasion for myself.' She pulled a face before continuing. 'Although I should have hated it – I am not comfortable being the centre of attention.'

There was no necessity to knock on the door as it was pulled open as they approached. Beth greeted them with enthusiasm.

'You are here at last; we have been ready this age. What do you think, Aubrey? Shall I be successful tonight?'

The girl spun about sending her gown swirling around her ankles. It was a pale pink with some sort of sparkly material over the top. 'I think you look quite delightful. Pink is perfect with your blonde curls.'

Giselle approached and curtsied as if he were a stranger. 'Do I pass muster? I do not wish to be outshone.' She opened her fan and fluttered it in front of her face whilst batting her eyelashes. 'You must tell me at once, my lord, that I am the belle of the ball.'

'You are a saucy minx, but a beautiful one. I believe that Beau and I will have our work cut out tonight fending off would-be suitors.'

She giggled and turned to show off her gown to Mary who was equally effusive with her praise. 'Yellow was an inspired choice, my dear; you and Beth look quite stunning. Shall we go down?'

Beth pointed at two pairs of pink slippers, and two pairs of yellow, neatly arranged on a chair. 'We have spare shoes to change into as we intend to dance every dance. As you know, Mary, dancing slippers rarely last the night.'

'I have never been obliged to change my footwear so was unaware of that fact. Although I must admit, I'm not overfond of dancing and rarely stand up more than two or three times.'

If she had announced she was the devil incarnate they could not have been more shocked. They could scarcely comprehend that any person could dislike dancing.

'Mary and I will dance together twice, and then no doubt she will take the floor with Beau. I shall dance with you two as well – but that will be the total of my performance in the ballroom.' He held out his arm and Mary placed her hand on it. The girls ran ahead, eager to be downstairs to see the changes to the reception rooms before they were obliged to stand in line to greet the first arrivals. He and his beloved progressed at a more decorous pace.

'Lady Johnson has agreed to come here and take care of the girls so we may both depart tomorrow as planned. I shall not leave until I have made sure everything is arranged as it should be. It's possible to complete the journey comfortably in one day so I hope that they arrive before noon. What time will you and your brother leave for Rye?'

She supposed that a member of the family must be in residence to greet Lady Johnson and her children when they arrived.

'We shall not set out before our guests are settled. Probably not until late afternoon; although it would be more convenient to leave at dawn.'

She smiled at his response. 'There is no need for both of us to be here – you have much further to go. I suggest that you and your brother depart at first light.' She pursed her lips. 'I do hope the duke doesn't think I am being presumptuous. It would be different if I was betrothed to him.'

'You would not suit, darling; you would be constantly at daggers drawn. He is not as malleable as I.'

Her delightful peal of laughter filled the hall. 'You are cut from the same cloth; you are as formidable as he. I would not be marrying you unless I was certain we were equally matched.'

His brother had been standing out of sight and overheard the conversation. He bowed to her and she curtsied in response. 'I hope that I am as fortunate as my brother if ever I go in search of a bride. That is a delightful confection, Mary. I shall be surrounded by a trio of beautiful young ladies this evening.'

'I believe I can hear the first carriage arriving. I had better find Beth and Giselle.' She paused and said quietly, 'I shall not, of course, be standing in the line. That is for family only.'

She vanished before either he or Beau could disagree. His brother shrugged and Aubrey nodded. She was right – if they didn't wish to reveal that they were betrothed then she could hardly be beside them. He had said he would not stand in line either, but knew he had no choice.

The front door was open and half a dozen maids were waiting to take any outdoor garments that might have been worn this evening. The footmen would be standing at the end of the red carpet that had been laid for this evening to lower the steps and assist the ladies from their carriages.

There was nothing Aubrey liked better than a ball. He was going to miss being part of the Season once he was married, but it was a small sacrifice to make in order to marry the woman he adored.

* * *

Mary discovered the girls admiring the floral decorations, banners and bows in the ballroom. The musicians were tuning up on the dais at the far end of the vast chamber, making it difficult to converse comfortably. Once they were outside Giselle grasped her hands in excitement.

'It looks so pretty – I don't believe I've ever seen this house look so well. Are we needed in the entrance hall?'

'Yes, the first of your guests are arriving. I'm relieved that I don't have to stand with you; it's going to take an unconscionable time for all two hundred of them to be welcomed formally. I shall mingle until you are released from your tedious duty.'

'You should be with us, Mary,' Beth said. 'You will be part of the family in a few weeks.'

'Remember, my dear, you must not mention this to anyone. It is a family matter at the moment.'

'I am so excited I could burst. Attending the assemblies at home count as nothing compared to this.'

'You must both be on your best behaviour tonight; every eye will be upon you, especially those of your brothers. Do not let me down. Also, Lady Johnson will regret agreeing to stay here whilst I am away if you misbehave.'

The girls joined their brothers as Lady Johnson and her five handsome children sailed in. Mary waited at the far side of the vast space to greet the woman who had now become a good friend.

'My dear Mrs Williams, how lovely you look tonight. I swear that you could be mistaken for a hopeful young debutante.'

'Thank you kindly for your compliment but I hope you are incorrect. I do admire your burgundy ensemble, my lady, and the turban with the three matching ostrich feathers is quite remarkable.'

Lady Johnson preened and nodded, making the feathers dance. 'It is a favourite of mine, my dear. Come along, children, I wish to find myself a favourable position in the ballroom before it becomes too cramped.'

As the room was empty she was able to select a group of gilt chairs grouped near the open French windows. 'This will be ideal. I can watch you dancing, and will receive a refreshing breeze from the door, and will be near enough to the entrance to the dining room to ensure we get an excellent table when supper is called.'

'A table has been reserved for us, my lady, so you have no need to worry about that.'

The youngsters asked permission to promenade on the terrace until the dancing started. Once they were alone Lady Johnson seated herself in a billow of silk.

'Our trunks are packed, my dear. I shall be here before noon. I cannot say that my children will accompany me so early, but they are quite capable of walking around from Hanover Square when they are ready. At what hour do you leave for the country?'

'I shall not leave until after you arrive, my lady, but the duke and Lord Aubrey will depart first thing. I have put the girls' itinerary on the escritoire in your sitting room. I'm sure that you have invitations to all the events that they have, but the final decision remains yours as to whether you attend any soirée, rout or ball.'

Mary had not given the true reason for Aubrey and Beau's departure. She had merely said that urgent business, involving their joint interests, was calling them away.

'We shall attend everything available – unless your girls decide otherwise. There's nothing I like better than being out and about seeing the world dressed in its finery.'

They talked of this and that for a further hour and by then the ballroom was becoming unpleasantly crowded. She saw Aubrey and his brother approaching through the crush. They were easy to spot being so much taller than most other gentlemen present.

'They are coming. The first dance will start at any moment.'

Aubrey saw her and his smile made her toes curl. She hoped nobody else had seen it. He arrived at her side and immediately apologised. 'It's taken the devil of a time out there; I've done enough bowing, smiling and nodding to last me a lifetime. I must lead Beth out in this first dance, sweetheart. I hope you forgive me. I should much prefer it to be you.'

'We are to dance the supper dance and one other, no more.'

She smiled as Beth glanced hopefully in his direction when the musicians struck up the first chord.

He strode towards the girl; she curtsied and he bowed. They made a striking couple, he dark-haired and she with golden curls. The duke and Giselle headed the set, Aubrey and Beth were next, and then half a dozen other couples hastily took their places.

There were a couple of gentlemen walking purposefully towards her, obviously intending to ask her to dance. 'My lady, I am going to take a turn around the garden. It is becoming unpleasantly hot in here.'

She managed to walk outside before she could be waylaid. There were a few older couples enjoying the warm evening breeze, but none of them were people that she knew. It would be foolish to venture onto the grass as it would be damp and ruin her slippers, and possibly the hem of her gown as well.

From her position by the balustrade she could see into the ballroom. There was a predominance of white and pastel shades, plus a sprinkling of colour from the older ladies. The gentlemen were dressed in black, but the occasional bright waistcoat added a welcome touch of colour. She was content to observe, enjoying the spectacle, but had no wish to be part of it herself.

Every time she spotted Aubrey her pulse quickened. He really was a most attractive gentleman.

20

Aubrey had no intention of dancing again with anyone apart from Mary but was obliged to partner his sister for the next set. He glanced across several times but his beloved wasn't there – she must have gone outside for a while.

He enjoyed prancing around the ballroom but he would much prefer to do it with the woman he loved. The musicians played the final note and the second country dance was over.

'I'm going in search of Mary; Giselle, do you have another partner in mind?'

'Excuse me, my lord, I believe this dance is mine.' Lord Rushton spoke from behind him. He was about to make an excuse for his sister when she smiled.

'Thank you, my lord, I should be delighted to dance with you.'

Aubrey stepped aside and watched as his sister was swept away on the arm of a gentleman he had not thought to see in the ballroom. Like Beau, Rushton preferred to play cards.

'Lady Johnson, do you have any notion where Mrs Williams has gone?'

The lady was fanning herself vigorously, her cheeks pink, and she looked uncomfortably overheated. 'I believe she went outside, my lord. I am awaiting her return so that I might take a turn in the fresh air.'

'Then I shall go and fetch her immediately,' Aubrey replied. He had no need to search as Mary stepped in from the terrace.

'I must take my turn as chaperone – poor Lady Johnson must be wondering what has become of me. I was watching you through the window, my love, and thinking how lucky I am.'

He guided her across the ballroom and her ladyship greeted them with effusion. 'Excuse me, my dear, I'm going to cool down outside. I shall not be above a half an hour.'

'Do you wish me to accompany you, my lady?'

'No thank you, my lord, I shall be perfectly well once I am outside. It might be beneficial if all the windows were thrown open – I cannot remember being so warm before.'

'If you will remain here, Mary, I shall find some footmen to do just that. It is remiss of them not to have done so already when the evening is so clement.'

'I am perfectly safe sitting here; there's no need to look so anxious on my behalf. There is only one other dance before the one that we are performing together. I sincerely hope that you are here for that.'

'I shall be back shortly – I cannot believe it will take me long to get some windows opened.'

In fact, it took him no more than a minute to deliver his instructions to a lurking servant. He was about to return to the ballroom when he was waylaid by his brother.

'You have just received a letter from Perry. I cannot think why it was delivered at this time of night but I thought you might like to read it immediately.'

'I certainly would. Will I find it in the study?'

Beau nodded. 'I told the footman to leave it on the desk. I

shall keep Mary company until your return – in fact I think I might dance with her.'

Aubrey smiled at the thought of his beloved's reaction to such a request after she had made it quite clear that she had no wish to dance with anyone but him.

The letter was where it should be. It was thicker than usual and he eagerly broke the seal and unfolded the two sheets of paper.

He quickly scanned the contents. He could hear his brother's voice in his head as he read. Perry had been given a new role to play – he was now attached to the intelligence officer. In future he would be incommunicado most of the time, behind enemy lines gathering information.

This sounded slightly less dangerous than leading a cavalry charge and a lot more interesting. He had already written telling his twin he was about to be married but the letters must have crossed as there was no mention of it in this missive.

He finished reading and replaced it on top of the desk so his brother could read it later. He would have liked to have bought his colours and become a dashing cavalry officer, but they had tossed for it and his brother had won the wager. They had decided it would be unfair to the family for both of them to risk their lives fighting the Frenchies.

The clock on the mantelshelf struck the hour and he swore under his breath. He was tardy. Supper was to be served at eleven and it was that time now. He had missed his dance and he thought Mary might well be annoyed with him for doing so.

He rushed to the ballroom expecting to see her sitting, tapping her foot, with Lady Johnson. She was not there; her ladyship was alone, nodding and smiling at the couples on the floor.

Then he saw his future wife being swept around the ballroom by none other than his brother. His eyes narrowed as he watched them laughing and talking gaily as if it were Beau to whom she was engaged. He recalled her comment earlier about such a thing.

* * *

'By rights I should be dancing with Aubrey, not you, sir.'

'If he had arrived in time to lead you out, then you'd be doing so. If I hadn't stepped in you would have been obliged to partner a stranger.' He smiled down at her. It was strange that he was, if that were possible, even more handsome than Aubrey, but his smile did nothing to upset her equilibrium.

'Then I thank you for rescuing me. I hope that your brother is as easily convinced of your good intentions – I have just seen him glowering at us from the edge of the ballroom.'

'I shall put things straight between us; never fear.' The music ended; he bowed and she curtsied. It was the custom for the gentleman to lead the lady he had just partnered from the dance floor and return her to her chaperone. Aubrey prevented this as he appeared at their side.

'I believe you have something that is mine, brother.' He was not smiling. In fact, he looked quite dangerous. The duke was not amused by this unnecessary confrontation. His arm tightened beneath her fingers.

'You forget to whom you speak...'

She would not be squabbled over as if she were a possession. She belonged to no one but herself. She interrupted them.

'Lord Aubrey, your grace, forgive me but I am feeling unwell. I am retiring immediately.' Allowing them no time to intervene, she stepped away and was lost to them in the press of people.

The back stairs that led directly to the guest wing might be a better way to go as Aubrey would expect her to use the main staircase. She picked up her skirts and scampered to her apartment – hardly the behaviour of young lady feeling out of sorts.

She leaned against her sitting room door expecting to hear his pounding footsteps approaching. After a few moments, the thundering of her heart subsided. He had not come and she wasn't sure if she was sorry or relieved.

Jessie had been given the night off so she would be alone and not have to explain her peculiar behaviour. As she would be travelling all day tomorrow she wasn't sorry she had left the ball early. The extra few hours of sleep would no doubt be beneficial.

After stepping out of her ball gown she shook it and carefully draped it over the wooden rack in the dressing room. It would need sponging and pressing before it was folded away onto a closet shelf. After completing her ablutions, she slipped on her nightgown and extinguished the single candle she had used.

The ensemble in which she was to travel the next day had been set out ready for her and there was ample water left for the morning. She had given instructions to her coachman to stop in Romford so they could find refreshments and allow the horses to rest.

The shutters were open, the window too, and when the music started again she would be able to hear it. She found it impossible to sleep and bitterly regretted her reaction to Aubrey's comment. She did not wish him to leave with bad feeling between them.

If she had not undressed so precipitously she could return and apologise. However, her hair was now in its night-time braid and she could never restore it to its previous arrangement without the help of her maid. Perhaps she should have been flattered that her future husband could become jealous, even of his own brother?

She tumbled from her bed and found her robe. She would

wait in the sitting room until all the guests had departed and then... and then what? She could hardly wander about the place in her night garments even at that hour.

If she penned a letter to Aubrey she could slip along to his apartment and push it under the door. He would find it when he eventually retired and this would put matters right between them. It would be preferable to apologise in person, but that couldn't be helped.

Quickly she scribbled the necessary words, sanded the paper, folded it and melted a blob of wax to seal it. Now would be the perfect time to venture out as any servants that were on duty would be downstairs. The ladies' retiring rooms were also on the ground floor, as was the one for the gentlemen. There was no danger of anyone seeing her if she delivered the note now.

By the light of her candle she saw the time was approaching midnight and she could hear the orchestra playing again in the ballroom. If she remembered correctly, there were to be four dances following supper and then everyone would leave.

She was just passing Aubrey's bedchamber door when she heard footsteps approaching. Without thinking she turned the handle and slipped inside. She must not be seen by whoever it might be.

The room was dark; the shutters and curtains had been drawn. She would remain here until she was sure the danger had passed. Then her bladder almost emptied when he spoke softly from behind her.

'My darling, you should not be here, but I am delighted you are.' He gave her no opportunity to explain why she was in his bedroom in her nightclothes. He scooped her up and she could not help but be aware that he was quite naked.

Now was the time to stop this – he would never do anything she didn't want. But her heart overruled her common sense and she reached out to bring his head down to her so she could press her mouth on his.

* * *

A considerable time later she was nestling, contented and blissfully happy, in his arms. She explained how she came to be in his room, but instead of laughing, he was horrified.

'I should have realised you would not have gone back on your determination not to anticipate our wedding night. We must be married immediately – I have the necessary document.'

'My love, there is no need. I should not have been wandering about the corridors in my nightwear. I could have said no, but I chose not to. I have no regrets. I love you and there's no need for anyone to know we have behaved so disgracefully. You are leaving first thing so I will say farewell now.' She was out of bed and scrambling into her discarded clothes before he could react.

'I shall be counting the hours until we are together again. Beau and I are riding to Rye; it's far too warm to be cooped up in a carriage.'

'It is a goodly distance to that port. You will have to overnight somewhere. If your brother wishes to ride my horse, then he has my permission to do so.'

'He has already made that decision, sweetheart. You know as well as I do that he asks nobody's permission for any of his actions.'

The bed creaked as he was about to clamber out. 'Stay where you are. I don't trust you not to try and persuade me back into your arms.'

'Goodbye, darling, take care of yourself,' he called softly from the bed.

Mary slowly opened the door and peered around it. The

corridor was deserted, the sconces doused. She could return to her own apartment without being discovered.

* * *

It seemed she had scarcely put her head to the pillow before the curtains rattled and Jessie was there to help her dress.

'Good morning, madam, and a fine, bright one it is too. Cook has asked if you would like a picnic box packed for the journey later so we don't have to stop at an inn if you don't wish to.'

'Unless we intend to relieve ourselves behind a hedge we shall have no option but to halt somewhere other than a field. Talking of food reminds me that I missed my supper last night so I am sharp-set this morning.'

Aubrey and his brother had departed long before she descended. She was pleasantly surprised to find both girls had come down to eat with her.

'I did not expect to see you before I left, but I'm delighted I can now say goodbye in person. Did you enjoy yourselves last night? Is Lady Johnson to expect a stream of callers this afternoon hoping to pay court to you?'

'I have not met a gentleman who takes my fancy,' Beth replied as she piled her plate with delicacies from the sideboard.

'And what about you, Giselle?'

Giselle blushed. 'I did spend time with someone that I quite liked but he is not interested in me in that way. Lord Rushton has known me since I was in the schoolroom and treats me as though I was a child still.'

'Then I shall leave for the country satisfied that neither of you are like to elope in my absence with someone unsuitable.'

They giggled at her teasing and the conversation turned to their plans for the next few days. The Johnson siblings arrived ahead of their mother, as eager as the girls to gossip about the previous evening. She was given a message from her ladyship that she must depart as planned; it appeared Lady Johnson had been delayed by an unexpected visitor.

* * *

The carriage was waiting in the yard at the back of the house. The time was a little after midday and the thoroughfare was busy with pedestrians and smart carriages. Having had so little sleep Mary dozed until the pace picked up and they got into the countryside.

'Shall I let down the window and open the blinds?'

'Please do that, Jessie; it is getting very stuffy in here.' She breathed in the sweet smell of untainted fresh air. 'I believe I should like a picnic after all; it's been far too long since I enjoyed the sunshine without the smell of smoke.'

She put her head out of the window and beckoned to one of the outriders and explained what she required. In a short while the carriage turned into a clearing away from the busy road.

'This is ideal. If you spread the rugs on the ground beneath those trees we can sit there in comfort.'

The horses were given water and allowed to graze. Not only had there been a basket provided for herself and her maid, but also another for the coachman, his assistant and the two outriders.

From her position Mary could watch the other vehicles as they travelled in both directions. What the passengers of these carriages thought of their *al fresco* meal she had no idea. After a pleasant interlude, she returned to the coach and the journey continued. They halted at six o'clock in Colchester at the Red Lion to allow the animals some respite.

'We should be at my estate in three hours as long as we don't suffer any mishap. My staff will be expecting us as one of the outriders went ahead to warn them of my imminent arrival. It has been far too long since I was here.'

'We were at Bentley Manor last September, madam.'

'So we were, but I only remained a few weeks before returning to help my mother with Miss Freemantle.'

She and Freddie had spent little time here during their marriage. However, the occasional visits had been enjoyable and she had no qualms about leaving his excellent staff to take care of things in her absence.

Where would she and Aubrey reside once they returned from their travels around the globe? She believed he had a substantial estate somewhere, so he would expect to be there. Bentley would become his, to do with as he wished, so she thought it might be expedient to inform the staff that she was about to become his bride.

It was full dark by the time they arrived but the welcome she received was up to her expectations. She was going to enjoy her short visit away from the noise and smell of London. She would have liked to write to Aubrey to tell him that she missed him, and ask him what he intended to do with this estate once they were married.

This, however, was impossible as they had neglected to give each other an address to which they could send any correspondence. It hardly seemed worth the expense to write to Grosvenor Square and then have the letter forwarded to somewhere in Rye. Quite possibly, by the time this was done they would both be back in Town.

Therefore, she would enjoy this brief visit, the last she would spend here as Mrs Williams, and not think about such trivialities.

21

Aubrey and Beau were in no particular hurry and had no wish to overtax their mounts by galloping across the countryside. A groom had gone ahead with their luggage on a packhorse, not only to reserve their overnight stop but also to arrange for refreshments mid-morning.

They trotted into the designated coaching inn after a pleasant morning hacking through the fields. Aubrey's stomach plummeted when he saw the groom was accompanied by someone else from London.

Beau reached him first. The man bowed and handed him a letter. His brother scanned the contents and handed it over. It was brief and to the point.

Beau, Aubrey,
   You must return at once. We need you most urgently.
   Your loving sister,
   Giselle

'Our horses have not been ridden hard. They have the

stamina to take us back. If we cut across country, but this time jump the hedges and ditches, we should do it in three hours,' Beau said.

'Thank God we watered them at the last stream we passed.' He was back in the saddle before his brother and heading at a dangerous pace for the open countryside. There was only one thing he could think of that would have made their sister write such a note. Something had happened to Mary. He should have killed Dunstan – he was certain whatever the emergency, this bastard was behind it.

He glanced over his shoulder to see if Beau was keeping up. He need not have worried. Cloud was a magnificent horse and could gallop for hours. He had the sense to slow his pace when they reached the neighbourhood in which they might be recognised. It would not do to draw unnecessary attention to the family.

It was late afternoon when they clattered into the stable yard. The horses were blown, and he and Beau were in little better state. He vaulted from the saddle and tossed his reins to a waiting stable boy.

Their approach must have been observed from the drawing room window as both girls were in the hall to greet him. There was no sign of Lady Johnson or her progeny.

Beth threw herself into his arms. She was sobbing, her words were incoherent, and he could do nothing but stoke her back and offer what comfort he could.

Giselle was with Beau and seemed to be making more sense. All four of them retreated to the drawing room and his brother closed the doors firmly behind them. This was an ominous sign.

'What's going on? Why have we been summoned back like this?' Aubrey demanded to know.

'Lady Johnson didn't come and a footman came to demand that everyone returned to Hanover Square,' Giselle said.

He gently took Beth to a daybed and she flopped onto it, still crying uncontrollably. There was little point in asking her what was going on – he would have to rely on Giselle who was more resilient and less emotional.

'Did she give any reason for her non-appearance?' Beau asked.

'This letter arrived and it was when we read this that we sent at once for you.' His sister handed over a crumpled piece of paper. He moved so he could read over his brother's shoulder.

Lady Giselle,

I regret to inform you that our acquaintance is at an end. I cannot allow my sons and daughters to be associated with a family upon which the most dreadful scandal is about to break.

Small wonder that Mrs Williams has taken herself off to the country before her disgraceful behaviour becomes common knowledge.

I shall say no more as you are too young and innocent to hear the sordid details.

How could the woman have discovered that Mary had spent the night in his bed? This was his fault. He had ruined not only the reputation of the woman he loved, but also severely damaged the family. He was about to apologise when his brother said something quite inappropriate for the drawing room.

The shock of hearing such language was sufficient to cause both girls to recover from their tears. 'I beg your pardon; I should not have said that. You must not look so stricken, girls. I have a good idea who is spreading the most pernicious rumours about Mary.'

Then Aubrey understood this scandal was nothing to do with what had happened last night. 'It's Bishop, Dunstan's friend, who is behind this. I thought it strange that things ended the way they did. We did not get Bishop blackballed or removed from any invitations and he will have been telling lies about what happened to Mary.'

Aubrey couldn't breathe. He was consumed by a white-hot rage and knew if he could find the perpetrator of this disaster the man would not survive the encounter.

'I'm going in search of him...'

Beau put a hand on his arm. 'Change your raiment; have something to eat before you go.'

'Very well. Thank God Mary had already left before this news arrived.'

'Beth and I have decided we wish to go home to Silchester Court. Our trunks are being packed and we intend to leave first thing tomorrow morning. You and Mary can get married immediately as you already have the licence. Whatever the gossip, once you are wed it won't matter.'

Aubrey was unsurprised by this announcement. 'I think that a wise move – better to let the dust settle before we venture out to any big events. Even if the gossip has reached Silchester, it will make no difference to our friends and neighbours.'

'We are going to spend the remainder of the day sending our apologies to those invitations we have accepted. I expect if we don't, we will have retractions arriving by the dozen by the morning. If Lady Johnson believes the worst, you can be very sure she will have spoken to all her friends and cronies,' Giselle said.

He and Beau left the girls to their task and headed upstairs for a much-needed wash and change of clothes. 'Do you intend to come with me?'

'Before we go we need to talk, Aubrey.' His brother accompanied him into his sitting room before continuing. 'If we are going to make enquiries at the club and at the coffee houses, we need to have our story straight. We don't actually know what the rumour is and until we do we cannot in all conscience set about putting things straight.'

'Why don't you send for Rushton? Although he doesn't have his own house in Town, I believe he is staying with his sister in Hanover Square.'

'Excellent notion – I shall put matters in hand immediately. We shall not set out until we have spoken to him.'

There was something Aubrey needed to say before his brother departed on his errand. 'Whatever happens, however damaged Mary has been by this, I am still intending to marry her. I believe you said to Bennett that Grace's ancestry would no longer matter when she became a member of the family.'

Beau threw his arms around him, which was most unusual as his brother was not usually so demonstrative. 'I don't give a damn what anyone says. As far as I'm concerned Mary is already my sister and has the protection of my name. Giselle is right – you must tie the knot as soon as we reach home. In fact, it might be better to do so before Mary hears the gossip as she might decide, as Grace did, that you would be better off without her.'

Aubrey's valet expressed no undue surprise to see his master return so soon. Perhaps he too had heard the gossip – after all news travelled faster amongst the servants than it did above stairs.

Stripped naked he stood in the hip bath so he could tip as much water over himself as he needed to. He did not linger in his dressing room and was ready to depart before his brother. A tray arrived from the kitchen and the appetising aromas wafting towards him made his stomach growl.

He demolished the food and enjoyed every morsel and hoped

a tray had been sent to Beau as well. He was impatient to be off but there was one thing he had yet to do. He took the back stairs and headed to the gun room. He intended to take the pistol with him this time and very likely use it if he came face to face with Bishop.

When he returned to the main part of the house his brother was waiting for him. 'Rushton is here. We shall talk in the study.'

Aubrey took one look at the man's face and his heart sunk. 'You look grim; tell me how bad it is.'

'It could hardly be any worse. Word is out that Mrs Williams is a hardened flirt who has somehow insinuated herself into your family with the intention of ensnaring one of you for herself. She was seen by someone when she arrived with just her groom for company at a posting inn. So the word of this person has appeared to confirm the vicious rumours that Bishop and Dunstan started.'

Rushton ran his finger around his neckcloth as if it had grown unaccountably tight.

'Get on with it, man, I need to know the whole,' Beau said.

'The substance of these rumours is that Mrs Williams was away from home for twenty-four hours in order to meet her lover, Sir Richard Dunstan. Word is that he left the country brokenhearted when she rejected him in favour of one of you.'

'Dammit to hell! I don't suppose it comes as a surprise to you, Rushton, that Mary and I are engaged to be married. This is an unmitigated disaster. If she gets wind of this she will never marry me, however much I tell her that once she is Lady Aubrey Sheldon she will be untouchable.'

'I fear that you are right. Rushton and I will go in search of the perpetrator – I think you must go at once to Silchester and somehow persuade her to marry you immediately. Don't wait for us to join you – you have Bennett, Grace, Carshalton and Madeline to attend the ceremony. That must do.'

He needed no further urging. He removed the pistol, powder and shot from the inside pocket of his jacket and handed them across to his brother. 'Here, you might well need these. Would you send word to my valet to pack my trunks and have them brought down with the girls' belongings tomorrow?'

'I shall do that before we leave. I wish you Godspeed and pray that you will reach her before the rumours.'

* * *

Mary was up and ready to take stock of her estate at dawn. As Bentley Manor was isolated, several miles away from the nearest village, there was no necessity for her to dress to impress. Instead she pulled on the men's breeches she had worn under her habit when she was following the drum.

She dragged on her riding boots, wound her night-time braid around her head and secured it with a handful of pins, and headed for the stables.

'Good morning, Mrs Williams. I have saddled Bruno for you. Are you riding astride or do you wish me to put on your side-saddle?' Jim, who fulfilled the roles of both head groom and head gardener, asked her.

'Astride. There's no need for you to accompany me; I intend to ride around to see what improvements have been made over the past few months and then shall visit my farms. As I shall be meeting the estate manager at Willow Farm, I will not be alone for long.'

After spending an informative and tiring day in the saddle she returned more than ready for an early dinner. There was no butler remaining at the manor as she had retained only half a dozen indoor staff and the same number to maintain the hundred acres of grounds that surrounded the place.

The housekeeper, Jenkins, was more than capable of keeping things immaculate and ready for occupation at a moment's notice. The housekeeper's husband acted as footman and they were ably assisted by four local girls who were quite happy to turn their hand to any task asked of them.

Jenkins was also the cook, and an excellent one she was too. There was never a formal meal served – far too much extra work. Instead, as always when she visited, Mary would eat in her sitting room upstairs.

Jessie had arranged for the bath to be filled and it was waiting for her. 'Exactly what I need – thank you for thinking of it. I don't intend to go downstairs again today so shall put on a morning gown.'

Whilst she was relaxing in the tepid, rose-scented water, her maid was busy in the sitting room laying up a table with the finest damask napery and silver cutlery. This always seemed an unnecessary fuss to Mary, but Jenkins wished her mistress to dine as her status demanded.

When she eventually emerged, the aches and pains of her day gone, Mary was more than ready for her dinner. She ate well and then settled down on the comfortable sofa to catch up with her correspondence. By eight o'clock she was yawning widely and decided to retire.

And so the next two days unravelled, each one running seamlessly into the other. The weather was warm, the sun shone brightly – in fact everything would have been perfect if Aubrey had been with her. Although she had only been here for half the allotted time she decided she would depart. The staff had been informed of her imminent marriage and assured their positions were secure.

Once the knot was tied she would suggest to her husband that they found a tenant for the house – it seemed a shame to have it languishing unoccupied. It was doubtful Aubrey would wish to spend any time in such a quiet backwater.

* * *

Aubrey galloped down the drive of Silchester Court, heedless of the shocked expressions of the gardeners and outside men who were working there. He had the sense to slow his horse's headlong pace before they reached the cobbled stable yard. He vaulted from the saddle and strode to the side door.

As soon as he stepped in, he knew there was something wrong. The house was too quiet – it had an unoccupied feeling to it. He ran into the drawing room and skidded to a halt. Every item of furniture was draped with holland covers. Mary was not here.

Peebles arrived in a rush. He bowed. 'We were not expecting you, my lord. I apologise...'

'I take it that no one is here?' The butler nodded. 'We are all returning from London now the ball is over. His grace, Lady Giselle and Miss Freemantle will arrive sometime tomorrow. Make sure everything is ready by then. I shall not be staying here myself. I've merely called in to give you the message.'

Although this was obviously untrue, Peebles remained impassive. 'Do you wish me to send a suitable footman to act as your valet whilst you change your garments, my lord?'

'No, I can manage perfectly well. Send word to the stable that I need a fresh horse saddled and waiting for me.'

He had stripped off his soiled clothes and was finding himself something fresh to put on when two jugs of hot water arrived. There was a tray of cold cuts, fresh bread, cheese and apple pie standing on the table in his sitting room when he emerged ready to depart.

Despite his foreboding, his spirits lifted a little at the thoughtfulness of the staff. He gobbled down the food and was back in the saddle in a few minutes. He would go to Bennett; his brother had been a soldier and would know what to do next.

Mary must have heard the gossip before she left for Silchester and decided to abandon him. He had no idea where to look for her and there was little point in him galloping all over the country until he had some notion of where she might be.

Bennett and his lovely young wife, Grace, were suitably shocked to hear of the unfortunate events that had taken place over the past few weeks. However, neither of them looked particularly dismayed that his beloved had vanished.

'I did exactly the same thing myself, Aubrey, but Bennett found me and persuaded me to change my mind. I'm certain you will be able to do the same with Mary. I must own that I am surprised that you fell in love with each other, but delighted you have found the person you wish to spend the rest of your life with.'

'That's all very well, Grace; Bennett knew exactly where you were. I realise now that I know very little about my future bride apart from the fact that she was married to Colonel Frederick Williams. I came here in the hope that you might be able to tell me something about the man that might help me in my search.'

22

Bennett frowned. 'I'm afraid I know nothing about Mrs Williams apart from what I learned when she was with the regiment. The best place to go would be the estate of her mother – I believe it to be somewhere in Somerset. I'm sure you will discover the information that you need in Beau's study.'

'Somerset? I doubt she would have gone there as she would be aware this would be the first place I would look. Think, man, did you never hear any mention of a property, somewhere the colonel intended to retire to when his soldiering days were done?'

His brother shook his head. 'I can remember nothing pertinent, but I have my journals somewhere in my study. They are not a complete record of my service in the regiment, but it's possible I jotted something down that might be of use to you.'

'I still think you should send a letter by express. Her mother will surely have knowledge of her daughter's whereabouts,' Grace said.

'I might as well wait until Beth and Giselle arrive tomorrow morning. I'm sure that Beth will have the information I need.

There is no need to alarm Mary's parent who, I believe, suffers from indifferent health.'

They agreed this was the most sensible option in the circumstances. As Mary already knew about the gossip, and that her reputation had been damaged almost beyond salvation, the need for urgency no longer applied.

'I had a letter from Perry just before all this blew up in our faces.' He told them the contents and they were both pleased to know his twin was doing well in his chosen career.

'Why don't you stay with us tonight, Aubrey, rather than rattle around on your own at Silchester?'

'Thank you, Grace, I should prefer that. I have been so preoccupied with my own problems I failed to enquire after your health. You certainly look radiant – being with child obviously suits you.'

'Now the pregnancy is more established I am feeling much more robust, thank you. I shall send a note to Madeline and invite them to dine with us as she is also blooming. There will be two new members of the family in the autumn.'

All this talk of infants was not to his taste, so he thought it better not to mention the fact that neither he nor Mary had any wish to set up a nursery. He was relieved when the conversation turned to plans for his wedding.

'I'm glad that all the family, apart from Perry, will be there to celebrate with you,' Bennett said.

'You both talk as if our nuptials will take place. I wish I was so confident. Mary is an independent woman; she will not easily be persuaded if she has made up her mind that marrying me will be the wrong thing to do.'

'I have every faith in your ability to convince her, Aubrey, but I must say that I have never known you so despondent, so lacking in confidence.'

'I think it is because she is a woman of experience, several years my senior, and is not as ready to follow my wishes as a younger woman would be. I love her and have no desire to marry anyone else but I am well aware it won't be a comfortable marriage for either of us.'

They exchanged glances and then Grace left him alone with his older brother. 'What I'm going to say, little brother, is something both Madeline and I have been concerned about. No, don't poker up at me – resume your seat and listen.'

'I know what you want to say and I have no wish to hear any criticism of the woman I love, even from you.'

'Good God, man, I've no intention of criticising Mary. We are all very fond of her, think of her as one of the family, but we have our reservations about... about her suitability as your partner. It's not her age, or her having been married before, but the fact that you are so different in personality and experience. We fear that she will be the dominant partner in your relationship and even though you might find it acceptable in the first flush of your romance, eventually you will resent her.'

Aubrey was about to contradict his brother but then said something else entirely. 'I love her to distraction, would be miserable without her, but I have to admit there is some truth in what you say. I have only known her a short time; you might say that this is hardly long enough for either of us to be certain that we will deal well together for the remainder of our lives.

'However, I shall not be dissuaded. She loves me as much as I love her and we will both learn to compromise. I appreciate your concern, but I wish to hear no more on this subject.' He stood up. 'You were told several times that Grace was unsuitable but continued in your determination to marry her. Do you think that I'm any different from you in that respect?'

His brother was now on his feet. They were of similar height, although Bennett was somewhat broader in the shoulder than he was.

'In which case, you have our unreserved support. We have been eating *al fresco* as the weather has been so clement and no longer bother to change for dinner.'

'Which is fortunate because I have no evening clothes with me. I must send word to Silchester that I will not be home tonight. I have already caused pandemonium by arriving when the dust sheets were still in place.'

They strolled into the garden to enjoy the late afternoon sunshine and discuss the price of corn, the progress of the war – in fact, anything that did not involve his relationship with Mary.

* * *

Beau decided to take a closed carriage despite the fact that with the weather being so warm, a gig or brougham would be more comfortable.

The inside of the vehicle was unpleasant but he wished to keep the blinds down so they would not be recognised.

'Are we to make enquiries quietly or walk into the club and make sure everyone present is aware of your fury at the malicious rumours? I heard from another gentleman residing in Albemarle Street, but he isn't a member of the *ton*.'

Beau shrugged. 'I think we must wait and see what greets us when we step in. If there is an uncomfortable silence, if heads turn in our direction, then we must go on the offensive. However, if things are as normal we take things quietly.'

'The club is only likely to have a handful of members present – the hardened drinkers and the bachelors with no establishments of their own. I think it highly unlikely Bishop will dare to show his face anywhere he is likely to meet one of us.'

'I don't expect to see him in person; I merely wish to ascertain his whereabouts and put a stop to the gossip. I've yet to come up with a sensible explanation for Mary's appearance at the inn that morning. Even a simpleton would know she would not have been riding in that area if she had come from Grosvenor Square.'

'You can hardly tell the truth. Being abducted and spending the night in captivity would be almost as damaging as what's being said already.'

'I'm certain that no one actually acquainted with us saw her there. I shall simply deny that Mary was away from home. I shall say it was a fabrication put about by Dunstan and Bishop to cause disharmony in the family. The motivation was revenge for having been ostracised by those he hoped to cultivate.'

'Why not mention the fact that your brother and Mrs Williams have been betrothed for a week? Say that she left Town in order to speak to her mother in person before returning to Silchester Court for the wedding.'

Beau considered this suggestion and then nodded. 'That's an excellent idea, old fellow. Now I come to think of it, I think it highly unlikely any of the *ton* will pay heed to this nonsense. I'll make sure that everyone is aware of Dunstan's intentions and his perfidious actions. I'm surprised that Lady Johnson, who I thought a sensible woman, believed these lies so readily.'

He reached out and banged loudly on the roof of the carriage. 'I have changed my mind. We must go to Hanover Square, the residence of Lady Johnson. We should have gone there first, Rushton. My wits are wandering today. I must own that my life was much simpler before Mary and my cousin joined the family.'

'It would make more sense for me to get out here and continue to the club. What do you wish me to do if I am able to locate Bishop?'

'On second thoughts, you continue in the carriage and I shall go on foot.'

The carriage rocked to a halt and the under-coachman scrambled down and opened the door.

'Thank you, I am going elsewhere. Take your orders from Lord Rushton.'

The man touched the brim of his hat. Beau jumped out without waiting for the steps. The door closed and moments later the carriage continued without him. His friend was a capable man. He had known him since they were up at Oxford together, and he could not have a better person aiding him in this business.

He was able to take a more direct route to Hanover Square than a carriage could have done and reached his destination within a quarter of an hour. He hammered on the front door. Only as he was waiting for it to be opened did it occur to him he might be turned away. Then he half-smiled. Whatever the circumstances, no one refused entry to a duke.

The door was opened by a footman. Beau stepped around him and strode into the house. Without turning his head, he held out his gloves, hat and cane and was unsurprised when they were removed from his hand.

'Conduct me to Lady Johnson. I am the Duke of Silchester.' There was no need to say anything else, to ask if her ladyship was receiving callers; he would not be gainsaid in this matter. He remained where he was in the centre of the entrance hall, looking to neither left nor right, his expression unreadable; it would be a brave servant indeed who disobeyed him.

'If you would care to come this way, your grace, her ladyship is in the small withdrawing room.'

The butler had silently arrived to take over from the footman who had opened the door. Beau remained where he was, which forced the man to step around him. He then followed, schooling his features, making sure he was every inch the toplofty aristocrat visiting an inferior.

Word must have been sent, as Lady Johnson was on her feet to greet him when he was announced. She looked terrified, and well she might, at his unexpected appearance. She dipped in a curtsy; he responded with a small nod, making it very clear of his status.

'Lady Johnson, you might well guess why I am here. Your behaviour towards my family is unforgivable and you will regret your actions before the day is done.'

He hated to cause her further distress, but if he was to discover why she had believed what she had been told he must remain austere and formidable.

'Your grace, I will show you. I received this letter as I was leaving for your house.' With shaking fingers she held out the missive. He remained stationary, forcing her to bring it to him.

My dear Lady Johnson,

When I heard that you are about to reside at Silchester House in order to act as chaperone to Lady Giselle and Miss Freemantle, I felt that I must inform you of some most distressing news.

Mrs Williams was seen by a relative of mine returning from a clandestine meeting with Sir Richard Dunstan. My cousin's butler is related to a member of Sir Richard's household and saw her there. Mrs Williams was overheard breaking off the liaison and saying that she intended to marry a Sheldon – that he was no longer good enough for her.

You must not allow yourself to be associated in any way with this woman as the scandal is about to break. You owe it to your sons and daughters to distance yourself.

The letter had been sent by an acquaintance and he saw at

once that bribery had been involved. He could also understand why the information had been believed.

'This explains why you behaved as you did. However, you have sadly mistaken the case.' He gestured towards a group of comfortable chairs halfway down the room.

'Shall we be seated, my lady? There are things I wish to tell you in confidence.' He smiled – she responded as he'd expected.

'Shall I send for coffee, your grace? Perhaps you would like a slice or two of cake to go with it?'

The last thing he wanted was cake, but he thought it would be expedient to agree. 'I thank you, my lady; that is exactly what I would like.'

When she had summoned a servant and given the order, she took a place opposite him and fussed about with her skirt. She was still nervous in his company, and he didn't blame her; he had behaved badly but family must come first.

'There is sufficient truth in what was said in that letter to make it sound authentic. However, I shall, in the strictest confidence, tell you what actually happened.'

He paused in his account to allow the footmen time to place the trays on a side table. Then Lady Johnson waved them away and they scuttled off, sending him nervous glances as they went. When he had completed the story she was wide-eyed and for the first time in their brief acquaintance bereft of speech.

'I've never heard anything so dreadful. And to think I blamed Mrs Williams – she will never forgive me.'

'If those to whom you told the contents of that letter are immediately informed that you were mistaken, then that should be enough to restore your friendship. The true story must never be revealed, but telling them it was someone else entirely that was identified at the inn as being Mrs Williams should be sufficient.'

'I shall do that, of course, your grace. I shall also make sure that they all are aware of the perfidious nature of both Mr Bishop and Sir Richard. They must both be fit for Bedlam to have behaved in such a way over so small a slight.'

He spent a further half an hour with the redoubtable lady and departed satisfied that Lady Johnson would do her best to put things right. However, it was doubtful things could go back to the way they were. Mary's reputation was irretrievably damaged, but hopefully once she was safely married to his brother it would be forgotten.

* * *

Mary left for London at dawn on the fourth day of her visit. Much as she loved the countryside she was bored with so little to do, and so few people speak to. Therefore, she had no option but to return to the smell and smoke of London.

The journey was uneventful and her carriage rolled to a standstill in the turning circle behind the house a little before six o'clock. If she recalled correctly, there was a fireworks party being held that night, so no one would go out until nine. Her first task would be to ascertain the exact direction of her beloved and send a letter by express asking him to return post-haste to her as she missed him dreadfully.

The grooms seemed surprised to see her – she should have sent word that she was returning early. Leaving her maid to organise the transfer of her luggage, she hurried to the side door. She was shocked to find it locked. There was no knocker on the door and she doubted if she banged with her fist anyone would hear in the servants' quarters.

She had no intention of going around to the front herself. She would send Jessie when she arrived. What was keeping the girl?

'Oh, madam, I've just learned that the house is closed. Everyone has returned to Silchester Court. The house is under covers...' Jessie dabbed her eyes with her handkerchief unable to continue. A lump formed in Mary's chest. She had a bad feeling about this.

'Go on, you must tell me everything.'

'His grace and Lord Aubrey came back the same day. His lordship left immediately; his grace, Miss Freemantle and Lady Giselle departed the next morning.'

'Then we shall follow them. We must stay here tonight and allow the horses to rest, but we will leave first thing in the morning. There must be some family emergency to have taken them away so suddenly.'

The side door was unbolted and she was ushered inside with profuse apologies from both the housekeeper and the butler. 'Send a tray to my apartment at seven o'clock. I shall require breakfast to be served there at six tomorrow morning. I wish a letter to be taken to Hanover Square. Send a footman to my sitting room to collect it.'

There was no need for them to bring up the trunks as they would be leaving again almost immediately. She found pen and paper in her bureau and quickly wrote to Lady Johnson in the hope that she might be at home and willing to call around and explain what had transpired.

She had given instructions to be fetched immediately if her ladyship arrived in person. She had scarcely time to complete her ablutions and tidy her appearance before she was informed her guest was downstairs.

23

Aubrey was prowling around outside awaiting the arrival of his family when his brother and Rushton cantered down the drive. He hoped they were bringing good news as he had spent another sleepless night. He was certain that the longer he was away from Mary, the more time she had to mull over what had happened, the more likely she was to remain obdurate and refuse to come back to him.

He waited on the front steps for the two horsemen to arrive in a flurry of gravel. They dismounted and handed the reins to the waiting grooms.

'Mary isn't here. She must have heard the gossip and run away. I need to speak to Beth most urgently. I'm praying she will know where I might find her.'

'I am bringing better news, but the fact that she isn't here makes things so much more difficult. The girls should arrive in an hour or two as they left at the same time as us, but we travelled more quickly.' Beau gripped his shoulder as he passed.

Rushton offered his hand and Aubrey shook it. 'I thank you for your help in this matter. There is a cold collation set out in the small dining room – you can both tell me your news whilst we eat.'

When he had listened to his brother's tale he was pleased with the outcome but was even more delighted with what Rushton had to tell him.

'I visited all the clubs of which I'm a member and only at one, White's, did anyone mention the gossip. Both gentlemen dismissed the rumours as poppycock and gave their word to make sure anyone who spoke about it was put right on the matter.'

'This makes me think that it's possible Mary hasn't heard anything detrimental to her good name, but is just visiting elsewhere. But where the devil is she? She could not possibly have gone to Somerset as she only intended to be away for a sennight.' Aubrey forked up another mouthful of the tasty beef pie that had been served to them and chewed.

'Wasn't she left a substantial estate somewhere by her first husband?' Beau said.

Aubrey threw down his cutlery with such force Rushton dropped his glass of porter into his plate of cold cuts. 'Devil take it! Of course she was. It's somewhere in Suffolk; I recall her mentioning it. I shall set off there immediately.'

'You can't charge away like a madman without having her direction. Suffolk is a large county – how do you expect to find it if you don't even know the name of the estate?' Beau asked.

'You are correct, of course, big brother. I might as well finish my luncheon.' He laughed at the mess he had inadvertently caused. 'I apologise for that, Rushton. Fortunately, there is plenty more for you to fetch.'

His good spirits were restored; he was certain he would find his love and they could get married as planned.

'They will be expecting us at Rye, Aubrey; I must send a letter by express with your requests and hope the captain is able to carry them out as you would wish.'

'Don't do that, Beau. I shall take Mary with me and she can have a say in how things are to be arranged for our travels. Of course, you must say that we are delayed, but make sure nothing is started until my wife and I arrive there.'

* * *

His brother and his friend decided to spend the afternoon playing billiards, but he was too eager to set off to settle at something so sedentary. Instead he walked around to the stables and told them he would need a carriage.

'I fear, my lord, that we will have no horses available for a team. The chestnuts are awaiting the blacksmith and I don't reckon he'll be here until tomorrow morning.'

'Then I shall ride – presumably you have a saddle horse I can use?'

'We do, my lord. Both the black and the bay are fresh as daisies and will take you anywhere you want to go today. The stable lad has just informed me there are two carriages on the drive. Will your valet, Wells, be accompanying you?'

Aubrey nodded. 'Have them saddled and ready for us in an hour.'

When the steps were let down on the carriage containing the girls he was there to hand them down. 'I'm glad to see you back. Mary didn't come here; she went elsewhere. Beth, can you tell me the name of the estate she was left by her husband?'

'Bentley Manor. I believe it to be in the neighbourhood of a town called Ipswich. The colonel purchased it, so Mary told me, as he had no wish to return to the family estate in Somerset. That was how he met Mary, when he attended an assembly when she was still living there.'

'Thank you, that's the information I need. Forgive me; I must speak to my valet. I intend to leave within the hour.'

The girls hurried inside, arm in arm, chattering gaily about how glad they were to be away from the crush and smell of the city. Giselle turned to him as they entered the house.

'Are the arrangements for your nuptials in hand, Aubrey? Do you intend to invite our neighbours or keep it a family affair?'

'Family only – but I should like to mark the occasion in some way. As the weather is so clement perhaps we could hold a garden party or some such thing. But you must do nothing until I have found Mary. It would be foolish to send out invitations and then have nothing to celebrate because she is not yet back.'

They agreed with this and he left them to their own devices. He found his brother and Rushton and told them he had the information he needed, and that he would be leaving shortly.

'It will take you two days to reach Suffolk, so we can't expect you back for a further three as you must allow the horses to rest. Therefore, assuming everything goes smoothly, we will require the curate to be here to perform the ceremony six days from now.'

Rushton was leaning on his billiard cue. 'Something has occurred to me, old fellow – did not Mrs Williams intend to stay away for a week? It is a two-day journey to London so she might already have departed before you could hope to arrive.'

Aubrey did a rapid calculation in his head and smiled ruefully. 'If she returns to Grosvenor Square she will find the house closed and immediately set out again for here. I'm beginning to think it might make more sense for me to remain where I am and not go gallivanting all over the countryside searching for her.'

'Go to London, little brother, and wait for her there. That way you can be certain you will not miss each other.'

'In which case, there's no urgency. I shall delay my departure until the morning.'

* * *

Lady Johnson was standing in the centre of the drawing room wringing her hands. Mary hurried across to her. 'Whatever is wrong, ma'am?' The story poured out and Mary wasn't sure if she was amused by the news, offended or relieved.

'Mrs Williams, I cannot apologise sufficiently for my part in this debacle; I contacted anyone who might have heard this malicious gossip and put them straight.'

'You must not distress yourself further; nothing has changed between us. I expect that his grace told you Lord Aubrey and I are betrothed and intend to get married immediately. I know you are in Town for the Season, but would you consider spending a week at Silchester Court so you could attend our wedding?'

'How kind of you to invite us after all that's transpired. A week in the countryside would be ideal. Are you certain his grace shall not object to you foisting us upon him at his ancestral home?'

'He will be delighted to see you, my lady. Consider this – it can only be to my advantage. When people hear you attended our nuptials that will just confirm that there was no substance in the rumours.'

They parted on good terms. Lady Johnson said she and her family would be ready to depart the following morning. They decided they might as well travel in tandem so Mary would wait until the Johnson carriage arrived outside.

It occurred to her that Aubrey would think her still at Bentley Manor and might well go there to locate her. There was nothing she could do about that. Her plans were made and she would abide by them. Another benefit of travelling with Lady Johnson was that their progress would be hard to miss.

He was an intelligent gentleman, would be able to do the mathematics for himself and work out that he would find her in London. Not for a minute did she consider the possibility that he might have changed his mind because of the gossip.

Lady Johnson sent word that one of the Johnson boys had not yet returned from his excursion to a prize fight in Romford. Mary could have left without her but decided there was no rush and so the departure was put off until after luncheon.

As she was making her way to the small dining room she heard the side door slam open and guessed immediately who had come in. She gathered her skirts and raced in a most unladylike way across the hall and threw herself into Aubrey's arms.

He was hot and sweaty, liberally covered in dust, but she cared not. He crushed her to his chest and she tilted her head to receive his kiss. A satisfactory time later he raised his head, but didn't release his hold.

'My darling, my life has been in turmoil these past three days, but now I have you here beside me all is well again.'

'I must tell you that I have invited Lady Johnson and her children to attend our wedding. I am very fond of her, despite her having misjudged me.'

'I think we have caused enough excitement for the staff, sweetheart. Shall we go elsewhere to continue this?'

His eyes were dark; his passion made her pulse race too. 'No, my love, we shall walk together and partake of the delightful buffet Cook has provided. I've no intention of misbehaving again before our wedding night – and certainly not in the middle of the day.'

They spent a happy hour discussing their future plans and

she was delighted to be included in the decisions to be made about the refurbishment of the yacht, which was to be their home for the next year or so.

'I believe I heard the Johnson carriage pull up outside. We must go if we wish to arrive in good time for dinner.'

* * *

When she stepped out of the carriage at Silchester she was greeted not only by the girls, but by the duke himself. He embraced her warmly.

'Welcome home, my dear, I cannot tell you how pleased we are to see you and Aubrey so content after all the unpleasantness.'

Beth waited until he had moved away and then stepped in for her kiss. 'Cousin Beau has said we can have a garden party. Giselle and I would dearly love to organise this for you as our contribution to your wedding.'

'Then so you shall. I doubt that you will be able to arrange anything elaborate in so short a time. Your brother is insistent that we marry tomorrow in your chapel and then leave the next day for Rye.'

Giselle arrived at her side. 'Fiddlesticks to that! It is your prerogative to have things arranged as you please and he must fall in with your plans. Beth and I have already written out the invitations to the party – it will be in two days' time.'

'What will be in two days' time?' Aubrey enquired as he slipped his arm around her waist.

'It would appear that we are having a celebration event whether we like it or not. This is going to take place the day after tomorrow, so we cannot leave before then.'

His sister put her hands on her hips and dared him to contradict. He laughed. 'That sounds quite delightful and if we remain for another day or two, it will make little difference.'

Giselle and Beth squealed with delight and hurled themselves at him. Mary hastily moved herself out of danger as he was kissed and hugged by the two girls. They ran off to set things in motion.

'When I married Freddie it was a rushed affair, again a special licence, but with no guests and it took place in the drawing room of my family home. He was being posted abroad and we add no notion of when he might be back so I had no choice but to agree.'

He took her hand and raised it to his lips. 'I'm so sorry, sweetheart, would you like us to postpone the ceremony? It will be torture remaining from your bed, but I shall happily do so—'

She interrupted him. 'I am content with how things are, my love. I've no wish to delay things. I doubt my mama would have come even if she had sufficient warning. Perhaps we could visit her before we set out on our journey?'

'Of course we can. It will take a week or two to get the yacht ready. Are you certain you don't wish to wait and have a more elaborate ceremony?'

'This will be quite different – we are marrying in a chapel with family and friends present.' She moved closer so no one could overhear what she was about to say. 'I realise now I was never truly in love with Freddie – I loved him, but what I feel for you is quite different. I can say with all honesty that if I could not marry you then I should never marry again.'

'I feel the same, my darling. Come, we must go in. My brother, his wife, my sister and her husband will be here any moment and we shall scarcely have time to change.'

* * *

Somehow everything was ready for the ceremony the next morning. There were sufficient people in the chapel, Beau believed, to make an occasion of his brother's wedding to Mary.

He had offered to walk beside her down the short aisle, but she had declined telling him there was no need as she wasn't a shy young bride but an experienced woman.

The Johnson clan were dressed in their finest, but looked uncomfortable in their position as the only non-family members present, apart from Rushton, of course. He wondered if by next spring there might be three, not two, babies in the family. For all their protestations that neither of them wished to have a child, he was certain if such a thing was to happen they would both be delighted.

The ceremony passed without any problems, the register was signed, and they all left the chapel and walked solemnly to the grand dining room, which had been decorated with ribbons, bows and vases of summer flowers.

Mary and Aubrey took the head of the table; he sat at the far end facing them. Lady Johnson and her five children, plus Rushton, took places on the left and the others sat on the right.

'I would like to welcome Mary to the family. Please raise your glasses to her.' Everyone stood and took a sip of the champagne that had been served in honour of the occasion.

There were further toasts before the first course was brought in. Giselle smiled at Mary. 'I hope you don't think we shall be dining in such splendour tonight. I have asked for a buffet to be served *al fresco*. In case you were wondering about tomorrow evening, Beth and I will tell you what is going to happen.'

The girls had somehow managed to obtain a stilt walker, a fire-eater, and a juggler, plus a quartet so there could be dancing on the terrace.

'We have arranged for a firework display to be set off on the far side of the ornamental lake to end proceedings,' his sister continued. 'Although we sent out the invitations at such short notice everyone has accepted. There will be around one hundred guests...'

'How will my staff cope with such a large number of unexpected arrivals? I sincerely hope you consulted with the housekeeper before setting things in motion, Giselle.'

'They have far too little to do. They are more than delighted to make a special effort in honour of Aubrey's wedding.'

Madeline joined in the conversation. 'You must not look so worried, Beau; everything will go splendidly. It would not dare do anything else with you in attendance. I know I spent a prodigious amount of time arranging the house party and all the other events last year. It's a far simpler task when there are no overnight guests and their staff to provide for.'

He nodded as if reassured, but he was certain there would be a dozen or more members of staff in the kitchen who would be obliged to work all night if everyone was to be fed. 'I know, Aubrey, that you and Mary will be leaving immediately the following morning and not able to attend, but I thought it might be a good idea to hold something less elaborate for the villagers, tenants and staff.'

'I think that would be much appreciated, Beau, and I'm sure none of them will object to the extra work involved,' Giselle replied.

There were three courses, each with several removes, and by the time the meal was done he had had far too much champagne and claret. When Mary rose the other ladies followed suit, leaving the gentlemen to drink port if they so desired.

'I'm a trifle bosky, little brother. I'm going for a walk around the park to clear my head.'

'I shall join you, Silchester,' his friend said.

Bennett and Carshalton said they were going to play billiards as their wives, being in an interesting condition, intended to rest until they regrouped for the evening meal outside.

Aubrey had drunk very little. He was the soberest of them all. 'Then excuse me, gentlemen, I'm going to find my wife and spend the afternoon...'

Beau raised his hand. 'There's no need to say more, little brother. We are well aware what you and Mary will be doing.'

The Johnson boys blushed scarlet and amidst much jollity the party dispersed.

* * *

Mary had no wish to drink tea or make trivial conversation. 'Please excuse me, everybody, I have had far too much champagne and need to lie down for a while. I shall rejoin the party in time for our outdoor supper. I'm relieved it will not be until seven o'clock – I doubt that any of us will be ready to eat again before then after such a delicious and substantial lunch.'

She made a show of clutching on to the door frame as if unsteady on her feet and then giggled (something she never did) hoping this behaviour would convince the watchers that she was indeed inebriated.

She had given Jessie the afternoon off so her apartment was deserted. Should she prepare herself for her husband's visit or sit demurely on the window seat reading a periodical?

There was no time to make a decision as he burst in. His smile was wicked; his eyes flashed his intent. In two strides he was by her. She was swept from her feet and he shouldered his way into her bedchamber.

He was as eager as she to consummate the union. 'Do I have

to undo all the laces and buttons on your garments or can I tear them off?'

'You will do no such thing, my love. I shall remove them myself whilst you take off your clothes.'

Watching him undress made her giddy with desire. When they had spent the night together she had not seen him in all his glory – it had been too dark. He was ready first but remained a yard away watching her every move.

When the final petticoat slithered to the floor she stepped out to stand proudly naked in front of him.

'I love you. This is the happiest day of my life.'

He closed the distance and tumbled her onto the bed. Needless to say, the delicious *al fresco* supper was eaten on the terrace without either of them being present to enjoy it.

* * *

MORE FROM FENELLA J. MILLER

The next breathtaking Regency romance in The Duke's Alliance series from Fenella J. Miller, *An Accommodating Husband*, is avail-able to order now here:

www.mybook.to/Accomm_HusbandBackAd

ABOUT THE AUTHOR

Fenella J. Miller is the bestselling writer of over eighteen historical sagas. She also has a passion for Regency romantic adventures and has published over fifty to great acclaim. Her father was a Yorkshireman and her mother the daughter of a Rajah. She lives in a small village in Essex with her British Shorthair cat.

Sign up to Fenella J. Miller's mailing list for news, competitions and updates on future books.

Visit Fenella's website: www.fenellajmiller.co.uk

Follow Fenella on social media here:

facebook.com/fenella.miller
x.com/fenellawriter

ALSO BY FENELLA J MILLER

Goodwill House Series

The War Girls of Goodwill House

New Recruits at Goodwill House

Duty Calls at Goodwill House

The Land Girls of Goodwill House

A Wartime Reunion at Goodwill House

Wedding Bells at Goodwill House

A Christmas Baby at Goodwill House

The Army Girls Series

Army Girls Reporting For Duty

Army Girls: Heartbreak and Hope

Army Girls: Behind the Guns

Army Girls: Operation Winter Wedding

The Pilot's Girl Series

The Pilot's Girl

A Wedding for the Pilot's Girl

A Dilemma for the Pilot's Girl

A Second Chance for the Pilot's Girl

The Nightingale Family Series

A Pocketful of Pennies

A Capful of Courage

A Basket Full of Babies

A Home Full of Hope

At Pemberley Series

Return to Pemberley

Trouble at Pemberley

Scandal at Pemberley

Danger at Pemberley

Harbour House Series

Wartime Arrivals at Harbour House

Stormy Waters at Harbour House

The Duke's Alliance Series

A Suitable Bride

A Dangerous Husband

An Unconventional Bride

An Accommodating Husband

Standalone Novels

The Land Girl's Secret

The Pilot's Story

You're cordially invited to

The Scandal Sheet

The home of swoon-worthy historical romance from the Regency to the Victorian era!

Warning: may contain spice 🌶

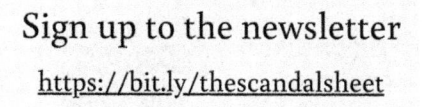

Sign up to the newsletter
https://bit.ly/thescandalsheet

Boldwood

Boldwood Books is an award-winning fiction publishing company seeking out the best stories from around the world.

Find out more at www.boldwoodbooks.com

Join our reader community for brilliant books, competitions and offers!

Follow us
@BoldwoodBooks
@TheBoldBookClub

Sign up to our weekly deals newsletter

https://bit.ly/BoldwoodBNewsletter

Printed in Great Britain
by Amazon